英文句型隨套隨用，
關鍵句型點 X 會話線 X 文法補充
讓會話實力再進化！

使用說明

Unit 01

There be (not)...

在中文裡我們常說的「有鳥在樹上。」或「有一個漂亮的女孩在那裡。」等等,都需要用到 there is 或 there are 的句型,翻譯成中文就是「有」的意思,是再基本不過的句型了!

關鍵句型點

❶「There be +代名詞或名詞(片語)+地點/時間」這是最常見並且超實用的一個句型,表示「某地(或某時)有某人(或某物)」。否定形式就是直接在 be 後面加 not,也就是:There be not...。

❷ There be 指的就是中文的「有」,其中的 be 動詞可以用各種時態出現,如現在式的 is、are,過去式的 was、were,未來式的 will be 等。

❸ 在這個句型中,主詞是代名詞或名詞(片語),所以 be 動詞要搭配主詞的單複數。如果句子中出現兩個主詞時,be 動詞的單複數要與最接近的主詞□□□□□□□「就近原則」。

❹ There be 句型還有□□□□□□□□□□開頭,交代故事發□□□□□□□be 動詞常用過去式

會話演練線

A Look! **There is** a beautiful girl.

B Really? Where?

會話翻譯

A: 看啊!那邊有一個漂亮女孩。

B: 真的嗎?在哪裡?

A I have no time to attend the singles party this weekend. What a pity!

B **There will not be** a singles party this weekend.

A: 我沒有時間參加這個週末的單身派對了,真可惜!

B: 這個週末並沒有單身派對。

A Once upon a time, **there was** a clever hunter living in the forest.

B Why do fairy tales always begin with "once upon a time"?

A: 很久很久以前,森林裡住著一個聰明的獵人。

B: 為什麼童話故事總是以「很久很久以前」開頭呢?

A Why aren't there any eggs in the fridge?

B Strange, **there were** two when I checked this morning.

A: 冰箱裡怎麼沒蛋了?

B: 奇怪,我早上看的時候明明還有兩個的。

Step 1 關鍵句型點

從最基礎的句型概念開始學起,告訴你句型的結構公式,先穩固「句型點」,了解句型的使用方法和時機,接著掌握時態變化和情境後,就能把英文句型運用自如。

Step 2 會話演練線

英文不能光說不練,必須要能應用才行。所以,將所學的句型概念,串成一條又一條的會話線,進行實戰演練應用,才不會學了功夫以後卻無處發揮。

Step 3 例句一連發

只練習句型和會話，或許不久後就會淡忘，但經過大量的例句轟炸、反覆練習後，絕對會讓你印象加倍深刻，所有重要概念通通想忘也忘不掉。

例句 一連發

❶ **There is** a gift in that box.
那個盒子裡有一個禮物。

❷ **There are** two fat men next to me.
有兩個胖子在我旁邊。

❸ **There will be** a party in the hall this evening.
今天晚上大廳裡將會有一場派對。

❹ **There isn't** enough food in the fridge.
冰箱裡沒有足夠的食物了。

❺ **There wasn't** a school sports game on the fi
yesterday.
昨天操場上沒有舉行學校運動會。

❻ Once upon a time, **there was** a beau
princess called Snow White.
很久很久以前，有一個美麗的公主，名字叫白雪公主。

❼ **There is** a beautiful girl standing there.
有一個美女站在那裡。

❽ **There are** 14 girls in our class.
我們班上有 14 個女生。

016

小小試身手

( ) ❶ There _____ a lot of people on the square every evening.
(A) will be　　(B) is
(C) are　　　　(D) was

( ) ❷ A: Oh! there isn't enough _____ for us in the lift.
B: It doesn't matter, let's wait for the next one.
(A) ground　　(B) floor
(C) place　　　(D) room

( ) ❸ Finish your food now. There _____ enough time for you to eat later.
(A) will not be　(B) will be not
(C) will not　　　(D) will be

Answer: C、D、A

❶ 句子的意思是：「每天傍晚廣場上都會有許多人。」這裡要注意的是時態，由題目中的 every evening 可以判斷這個句子是現在式，所以 be 動詞要用現在式 is 或 are。但主詞 people 是可數名詞複數形式，所以 be 動詞要也用複數形式 are。答案是 (C)。

❷ 句子的意思是：「噢！電梯裡沒有足夠的地方給我們了。」「沒關係，我們等下一班吧！」這裡要注意的是句子中所用的 be 動詞是 is，所以主詞必須是單數或不可數名詞，room 有「空間」的意思，最_____符合題目的要求，所以答案是 (D)。

_____食物吃完，待會你不會有時間吃的。」_____時間吃，那就不必現在急著吃完，因_____刪除。剩餘答案中，(A) 為 there be _____式，為正確答案。

017

Step 4 小小試身手

趁著記憶還十分清晰時，將剛剛好不容易弄懂的「句型點」、「會話線」，打鐵趁熱複習一遍，透過自我檢測的方式練習，能最快速檢視學習成果。

Level 1

過關大挑戰

1 ____lots of children on the square.
(A) There is
(B) We h
(C) There are
(D) It has

2 ____ice and water all over the forest afte
(A) It has
(B) There
(C) There are
(D) They

3 A: Would you please lend some money t
B: ____. Here you are.
(A) Yes, I would
(B) No, I
(C) Certainly
(D) No, I'

4 A: What's the climate ____ there?
B: It's very pleasant.
(A) X
(C) look like
(B) like
(D) look

5 Let's have a party, ____ ?
(A) will you
(C) will we
(B) shall
(D) have

6 Would you like ____ some juice? ____
(A) X / Yes, I'd like some coffee (B) X / No
(C) have / Yes, thanks
(D) to ha

058

超詳細解析

1 There be 句型表示「某地有某物／某人」。be 動詞要與主詞的單複數一致，而主詞 children 是可數名詞 child 的複數形式，所以 be 動詞要用 are，答案選 (C)。

2 首先確認要用 There be 句型。其次，這裡的主詞有兩個，分別是 ice 和 water，而 be 動詞要遵循「就近原則」，所以根據不可數名詞 ice，可知 be 動詞要用 is，所以選 (B)。

3 Would you please...? 這個句型用於向某人提出詢問、請求，意思是「你可以……嗎？」或「可不可以請你……？」。Would 在這裡並不表示過去時態，而表示更加委婉和客氣的請求。回答這個句型時，如果願意，可以說 Yes, I'll be glad to. / Certainly. / Of course. 等；如果不願意或不能夠，可以說 No, I'm sorry. / Sorry, but... 等。但據後面的 Here you are（給你）可以判斷，回答者是願意借錢給對方的，所以應該用 Certainly「當然可以」，選 (C)。

4 What is ...like? 這個句型可以用來詢問天氣、氣候。What is + 名詞 ...? 則是用來詢問某物「是什麼」或某人的職業、職務或社會地位等「是什麼」。look like 放在 what 疑問句中前面要用助動詞 does，即 What does...look like?，因此答案為 (B)。

5 當句子前半部是 Let's 時，表示說者提出的請求和建議也是針對聽者的，聽者亦參與其中。換句話說，說者和聽者雙方都參與這個建議內容，因此附加問句要用 shall we，答案選 (B)。

6 句型 Would you like...? 表示「你想要……嗎？」，用來表示禮貌的請求、建議，或詢問對方是否需要什麼，或徵求意見與看法。like 後面可以接名詞或代名詞，也可以接不定詞。但是在回答時，如果是肯定，就用 Yes, please；如果是否定的，就用 No, thanks，所以選 (D)。

7 How about...? 用來徵求意見、詢問消息或提出建議，意思是「……怎麼樣？」在這個句型中 about 後面不能接不定詞或原形動詞，而要接名詞或動名詞，所以以後面的 go 要改成動名詞形式 going traveling。所以選 (C)。

8 這裡要注意的是句型 How long...? / When...? / How soon...? / How often... ? 之間的不同。用 How often 是詢問「多久做某事一次？」；When 是詢問「什麼時候？」；How soon 表示從現在起的「多久以後？」；這三個選項都不符

060

全書共分為六個 level，每當要進入下個 level 前，最好都來個過關測驗看看自己的能耐，徹底檢視自己的能耐，才不會越級打怪，越學越沒有自信！

Level 1 補充文法面

瞭解 5 種主要詞性，破解 5 大基本句型

英文句型與英文文法的關係密不可分，所以在開始學習句型之前，我們先來複習幾個簡單的文法概念，這些文法概念可以幫助你學習句型，很快的掌握學習重點。首先，我們先來瞭解英文文法的詞性，最主要的詞性可以分為：

1 名詞

在英文裡，名詞可以分為可數名詞和不可數名詞，例如一顆一顆數得出來的蘋果（apple）就是可數，而像水（water）這樣的東西就是不可數名詞。另外，針對可數名詞來說，又可以分為單數名詞和複數名詞，如前面所講的蘋果（apple），它的單數就是 apple，複數就是 apples。

2 代名詞

代名詞顧名思義就是代替名詞的詞，也就是說，當我們不想說出名詞時，就可以用代名詞代替，例如剛剛所提到的名詞 apple，單數 apple 的代名詞就是 it，而複數 apples 的代名詞就是 they。

3 動詞

動詞可說是一個句子當中的靈魂人物，它可以幫助句子動起來，例如：run（跑）、fly（飛）、eat（吃）……等描述動作的單字都算是動詞。另外還有一種所謂的 be 動詞，中文通常翻譯成「是」，例如 am、are、is 等都是。

4 形容詞

在一個句子當中，形容詞所扮演的角色其實是用來襯托名詞的，如果名詞是主角，形容詞就是配角；如果名詞是新娘，形容詞就是伴娘。再以剛剛所提到的 apple 來解釋，apple 是名詞，而 red（紅色的）就是用來形容 apple 的形容詞，即 a red apple（一顆紅色的蘋果）。

5 副詞

副詞在句子當中所扮演的是修飾動詞的角色，例如剛剛所說的動詞 run（跑）、fly（飛），如果我們要進一步修飾動詞，可以說「跑得快」（run fast）、「飛得高」（fly high），fast 和 high 都是所謂的副詞。

瞭解名詞、代名詞、動詞、形容詞、副詞這五個主要的詞性之後，我們就要開始進入句型的主題了。雖然英文句型看起來既多又複雜，但其實我們最常用的句型不外乎下列五種：

① S + V   **④** S + V + O + O
② S + V + SC   **⑤** S + V + O + OC
③ S + V + O

看到上面密密麻麻的英文字你一定嚇壞了，不用擔心，接下來我們會一一介紹每個句型中，英文字母所代表的含意，看完我們的解說後，你就會發現一點都不難。

1. S（主詞）：

主詞是句子當中「做出動作」的人或物，例如：在 Birds fly.（鳥飛）這個句子中，我們先找出動詞 fly（飛），然後再看看是誰在飛，發現是 Birds 在飛，所以 Birds 就是這個句子當中的主詞。

Step 6 補充文法面

認真的你，在克服「句型點」、「會話線」之後，怎麼能夠不再更進一步對文法下戰帖呢！全書 6 篇文法補充，讓你點線面得以全方位強化，徹底攻克英文！

Preface 前言

　　學習英文，單字的重要性絕對是無庸置疑的，它是最基本的元素，一個人的單字量如果太少，就沒有辦法順利表達，因此大家對「記單字」這件事絕對不會馬虎看待；而文法的重要性更是不由分說，少了文法，一種語言就失去了它最主要的架構，猶如一艘船沒了龍骨，肯定一下就會支離破碎，所以，大部份的人即便再討厭文法，最後仍會乖乖地含淚苦讀它。

　　那麼「句型」呢？句型在英文學習中有什麼重要？是不是不學句型也沒關係？

　　鑑於對句子產生恐懼的學生數量越來越多，我和我英語團隊的老師們開會討論後決定撰寫一本解決學生害怕長句子問題的句型書。

　　本書將平時生活中最常出現、使用頻率最高的 72 種句型彙集成冊，再將這 72 種句型分為 6 大類，從點到線、從線到面地融會貫通英文概念，為的就是讓你能夠一本戰勝句型，克服「英文句子恐懼症」，往後看到再長的句子都可以直覺反應一秒看懂，無論聽說讀寫都能運用自如，這才是真正攻頂、征服英文的不二法門！

Contents 目錄

Level 1

Level 2

Level **3**

Level **4**

Level 5

Level 6

Level **1**

Unit 01

There be (not)...

在中文裡我們常說的「有鳥在樹上。」或「有一個漂亮的女孩在那裡。」等等,都需要用到 there is 或 there are 的句型,翻譯成中文就是「有」的意思,是再基本不過的句型了!

 關鍵句型

❶ 「There be ＋代名詞或名詞(片語)＋地點/時間」這是最常見並且超實用的一個句型。表示「某地(或某時)有某人(或某物)」。否定形式就是直接在 be 後面加 not,也就是:There be not...。

❷ There be 指的就是中文的「有」,其中的 be 動詞可以用各種時態出現,如現在式的 is、are,過去式的 was、were,未來式的 will be 等。

❸ 在這個句型中,主詞是代名詞或名詞(片語),所以 be 動詞要搭配主詞的單複數。如果句子中出現兩個主詞時,be 動詞的單複數要與最接近的主詞一致,即遵循「就近原則」。

❹ There be 句型還有一個很常用的場合,那就是用於故事發生的開頭,交代故事發生的時間。此時,因為是在講述故事,所以 be 動詞常用過去式,而且還常與過去時間副詞連用。

會話演練 **線**

會話翻譯

A Look! **There is** a beautiful girl.

B Really? Where?

A: 看啊！那邊有一個漂亮女孩。

B: 真的嗎？在哪裡？

A I have no time to attend the singles party this weekend. What a pity!

B **There will not be** a singles party this weekend.

A: 我沒有時間參加這個週末的單身派對了，真可惜！

B: 這個週末並沒有單身派對。

A Once upon a time, **there was** a clever hunter living in the forest.

B Why do fairy tales always begin with "once upon a time"?

A: 很久很久以前，森林裡住著一個聰明的獵人。

B: 為什麼童話故事總是以「很久很久以前」開頭呢？

A Why aren't there any eggs in the fridge?

B Strange, **there were** two when I checked this morning.

A: 冰箱裡怎麼沒蛋了？

B: 奇怪，我早上看的時候明明還有兩個的。

例句 一連發

❶ **There is** a gift in that box.
那個盒子裡有一個禮物。

❷ **There are** two fat men next to me.
有兩個胖子在我旁邊。

❸ **There will be** a party in the hall this evening.
今天晚上大廳裡將會有一場派對。

❹ **There isn't** enough food in the fridge.
冰箱裡沒有足夠的食物了。

❺ **There wasn't** a school sports game on the field yesterday.
昨天操場上沒有舉行學校運動會。

❻ Once upon a time, **there was** a beautiful princess called Snow White.
很久很久以前,有一個美麗的公主,名字叫白雪公主。

❼ **There is** a beautiful girl standing there.
有一個美女站在那裡。

❽ **There are** 14 girls in our class.
我們班上有 14 個女生。

小小 試身手

( ) ❶ There _____ a lot of people on the square every evening.
(A) will be   (B) is
(C) are   (D) was

( ) ❷ A: Oh! there isn't enough _____ for us in the lift.
B: It doesn't matter, let's wait for the next one.
(A) ground   (B) floor
(C) place   (D) room

( ) ❸ Finish your food now. There _____ enough time for you to eat later.
(A) will not be   (B) will be not
(C) will not   (D) will be

Answer: C、D、A

❶ 句子的意思是：「每天傍晚廣場上都會有許多人。」這裡要注意的是時態，由題目中的 every evening 可以判斷這個句子是現在式，所以 be 動詞要用現在式 is 或 are。但主詞 people 是可數名詞複數形式，所以 be 動詞要也要用複數形式 are。答案是 (C)。

❷ 句子的意思是：「噢！電梯裡沒有足夠的地方給我們了。」「沒關係，我們等下一班吧！」這裡要注意的是句子中所用的 be 動詞是 is，所以主詞必須是單數或不可數名詞，room 有「空間」的意思，是不可數名詞，符合題目的要求，所以答案是 (D)。

❸ 句子的意思是：「現在就把食物吃完，待會你不會有時間吃的。」由常理推測，如果待會有時間吃，那就不必現在急著吃完，因此表示「會有」的 (D) 可刪除。剩餘答案中，(A) 為 there be not... 句型未來式的正確形式，為正確答案。

主詞 sound/feel/taste/look/ smell (like)...：感官動詞

中文裡常說的「聽起來很不錯」或「看起來很漂亮」等，都是運用到眼、耳、鼻、舌等感官來描述某樣東西，在英文裡就是用 sound, feel, taste, look, smell 等感官動詞來表現。

 關鍵句型 **點**

❶ 這個句型的關鍵在於感官動詞，常見的感官動詞有 sound（聽起來）, feel（感覺起來）, taste（嚐起來）, look（看起來）, smell（聞起來）。這五個感官動詞後面常接形容詞、名詞，來說明主詞所處的狀態，即：「主詞 ＋ sound/feel/taste/look/ smell ＋形容詞／名詞」。除了 look 以外，其他幾個感官動詞的主詞往往是物，而不是人。

例 You **look** pale. →你看起來很蒼白。

❷ 感官動詞也經常和 like 連用，like 是介系詞，意思是「像……」，後面要接名詞，即：「主詞 ＋ sound/feel/taste/look/smell ＋ like ＋名詞」，其意思是「聽起來／摸起來／嚐起來／看起來／聞起來像……」

例 It **sounds like** birds. →這聽起來像鳥鳴。

會話演練 **線**

會話翻譯

A Why don't you have more soup?

B The soup **tastes** too sour.

A: 你為什麼不多喝一點湯呢？

B: 那湯喝起來太酸了。

A You **look** pale. What's wrong with you?

B I have a stomachache.

A: 你的臉色看起來很蒼白，你怎麼了？

B: 我胃痛。

A Do you like the music?

B Yes, it **sounds like** birds.

A: 你喜歡這首曲子嗎？

B: 喜歡，這首曲子聽起來像鳥鳴。

A I **feel** sick.

B Do you want me to tell the driver to slow down?

A: 我覺得不太舒服。

B: 要我叫司機開慢一點嗎？

例句一連發

❶ He looks tired.
他看起來很累。

❷ It feels like rain.
感覺要下雨了。

❸ It sounds like a train going under my room.
（那個聲音）聽起來像是火車從我的房間下開過。

❹ Silk feels very smooth and soft.
絲綢摸起來又光滑又柔軟。

❺ Swiss chocolate tastes wonderful.
瑞士巧克力嚐起來味道好極了。

❻ This flower smells good.
這朵花聞起來很香。

❼ Her idea sounds like fun.
她的主意聽起來很有趣。

❽ It sounds like a reasonable excuse.
這聽起來是個很合理的藉口。

小小試身手

( ) **❶** The story sounds_____ .
(A) to be true (B) as true
(C) being true (D) true

( ) **❷** A: This drink tastes _____ and it tastes _____ orange juice.
B: But in fact it is mango juice.
(A) sweet / X (B) sweetness / X
(C) sweet / like (D) sweetly / like

( ) **❸** You look _____. What's up?
(A) gladly (B) happily
(C) happy (D) sadly

Answer: **D、C、C**

❶ 句子的意思是「這故事聽起來是真的。」這裡要注意的是感官動詞 sound 的後面要接形容詞，而這裡只有 true 是形容詞，因此答案是 (D)。

❷ 句子的意思是「這飲料嚐起來很甜，且味道像柳橙汁。」「但實際上它是芒果汁。」這裡要注意的是感官動詞 taste 後面要接形容詞，所以第一個空格要填形容詞 sweet。而第二個空格之後接的是名詞「柳橙汁」，可見 taste 後面一定接了 like，意思是「嚐起來像……」，所以答案選 (C)。

❸ 句子的意思是「你看起來很開心。怎麼了？」感官動詞後面要接形容詞而非副詞，選項中唯一的形容詞 (C) 為正確答案。

Unit 03

What is/does... like?

在中文裡，當我們說「你男朋友怎麼樣啊？」時，表示我們想知道對方男朋友的外表、性格、生活等各方面的情形，在英文裡就是用這個句型來表示。

關鍵句型 點

❶「這個句型可以分為 What is...like? 和 What does...look like?。大致來說，這兩個句型都是用來詢問「……是什麼樣子？」其中的 like 是介系詞，表示「像」。不過它們也有以下區別：What is...like? 既可以詢問人也可以詢問事物。對人詢問的是人的性格、能力或給人的印象等；對事物詢問的是性質、特徵、特定情況等，有時甚至需要做詳細的描述。另外，What is...like? 也可以詢問外表。

 What is her boyfriend **like**? →她的男朋友怎麼樣？

What is the climate **like** in your hometown?
→你家鄉的氣候怎麼樣啊？

What's your job **like**? →你的工作怎麼樣？

❷ What does...look like? 意為「看起來……是什麼樣子？」、「看起來怎麼樣？」只用來詢問某人或某物的外部特徵。

 What does your boss **look like**? →你的老闆長得怎麼樣？

會話演練 **線**

會話翻譯

A **What is** her boyfriend **like**?
B He is honest and clever.

A: 她男朋友怎麼樣啊？
B: 他誠實又聰明。

A **What is** the climate **like** in your hometown?
B It's not too hot and not too cold.

A: 你家鄉的氣候怎麼樣啊？
B: 不會太冷也不會太熱。

A **What does** your boss **look like**?
B He is tall and thin.

A: 你的老闆長得怎麼樣？
B: 他又高又瘦。

A **What's** your job **like**?
B It's very easy and boring.

A: 你的工作怎麼樣啊？
B: 非常簡單而且無聊。

A **What do** your sisters **look like**?
B They look exactly like me.

A: 你的妹妹們長什麼樣子？
B: 她們長得跟我一模一樣。

例句**一連發**

❶ **What does** this building **look like**?
這幢大樓看起來是什麼樣子？

❷ I have never seen your brother. **What is** he **like**?
我從未見過你弟弟。他人怎樣？

❸ **What does** your sister **look like**?
你姊姊長什麼樣子呢？

❹ —**What does** the moon **look like**?
　—It's big and round.
一月亮長什麼樣子呢？
一它又大又圓。

❺ —**What is** the weather **like** tomorrow?
　—The weatherman said it would rain.
一明天的天氣怎麼樣呢？
一氣象預報員說會下雨。

❻ **What** is your life **like**?
你的生活過得怎麼樣呢？

小小**試身手**

( ) **❶** –What's the weather _____ in London?
 –It is foggy, rainy and seldom sunny.
 (A) X (B) like
 (C) look like (D) look

( ) **❷** –What does the man _____?
 –He is tall and thin and very badly dressed.
 (A) look (B) like
 (C) look like (D) be like

( ) **❸** –_____ your boss like?
 –He's pretty nice most of the time.
 (A) What does (B) What is
 (C) What do (D) How does

Answer: **B、C、B**

❶ 句子的意思是「倫敦的天氣怎麼樣？」「霧濛濛、多雨，很少有晴天。」根據句子的意思以及對話的內容可以得知這裡是問天氣，所以只能用 What is...like? 這個句型。如果要選 look like，則 what 後面應該要接 does，即 What does...look like? 所以本句不能選 (C)，因此答案是 (B)。

❷ 句子的意思是「那個男人看起來怎麼樣？」「他又高又瘦，穿著很差勁。」這個句子主要詢問別人的長相。因為問句以 What 為疑問句，而且助動詞是 does，所以後面要接 look like（看起來像），因此答案選 (C)。

❸ 句子的意思是：「你的老闆是什麼樣子？」「他大部分的時間人都不錯。」後句回答者說的是老闆的個性而非他的長相或喜好，因此選擇表達「他這個人怎麼樣」的 (B) 為正確答案。要是選了 (A)，就變成在問「老闆喜歡什麼」了。

Unit 04

Would you like...?

當我們想詢問別人的意願時，如：「你想不想一起去野餐呢？」或「你要不要喝點東西？」，就是用這個句型。

 關鍵句型 **點**

❶ Would you like...? 意為「你想要……嗎？」用來表示禮貌的請求、建議，或詢問對方是否需要什麼，或徵求意見與看法。回答時，如果是肯定，就用 Yes, please.；如果是否定，就用 No, thanks.。根據 like 後面接的詞語不同，又可分為以下兩種搭配，第一種是：「Would you like ＋名詞／代名詞？」就是 like 後面直接接名詞、代名詞或名詞片語。

例 **Would you like** a ride? →你想要我載你一程嗎？
　　Would you like some tea? →你想喝點茶嗎？

「Would you like to do...?」就是 like 後面接不定詞。

第二種是：

例 **Would you like** to have a drink after work?
　　→下班後去喝一杯怎麼樣？

❷ 另外一個延伸句型是：What would you like (＋ ...)? 這句話常用在餐廳點餐時，意思是「你想要點什麼？」如果想要說「你想要喝點或點些什麼？」則在 like 後面加上 to drink 或 to order 即可；而如果想要具體詢問對方某一餐想要點什麼，則在 like 後面接「for+ 三餐」即可。

例 **What would you like** to order, sir?
　　→您想要點些什麼呢，先生？

會話演練 **線**

會話翻譯

A **What would you like** to order, sir?	A: 先生，你想要點什麼？
B I'd like to try some Chinese food.	B: 我想嚐嚐中國菜。

A **Would you like** to have a drink after work?	A: 下班後去喝一杯怎麼樣？
B I'm afraid I'm busy tonight.	B: 恐怕我今天晚上會很忙。

A **Would you like** a ride?	A: 你想要我載你一程嗎？
B Yes, I'll appreciate it very much.	B: 是的，太感激了。

A **Would you like** some tea?	A: 你想喝點茶嗎？
B No, Thanks. I'd prefer coffee.	B: 不，謝謝。我比較喜歡喝咖啡。

A **What would you like** for dinner?	A: 晚餐你想吃什麼？
B I'd like some bread and sausages.	B: 我想要一些麵包和香腸。

例句一連發

❶ Would you like some water?
你想要喝點水嗎？

❷ Would you like to play basketball with us?
你想和我們一起去打籃球嗎？

❸ Would you like one of these moon cakes?
你想要一塊這樣的月餅嗎？

❹ What would you like for breakfast?
你早餐想吃點什麼？

❺ —Would you like to go mountain-climbing tomorrow?
　—I'd like to.
　—你明天想去爬山嗎？
　—我想去。

❻ Would you like to take these two suitcases to Tom?
你願意把這兩個行李箱帶給湯姆嗎？

小小**試身手**

( ) **1** –Would you like _____ some more salad?
　　 –_____ I am full.
　　 (A) to eat / Yes, please.　　(B) eat / Yes, please.
　　 (C) X / No, thanks.　　(D) eat / No, thanks.

( ) **2** –Would you like to come to the party tonight?
　　 –_____ but I am too busy today.
　　 (A) Yes, I'd like to.　　(B) Yes, I like it.
　　 (C) No, I don't.　　(D) I like to.

( ) **3** –Would you like to go hiking?
　　 –_____
　　 (A) Sure, when?　　(B) Yes, I like it very much.
　　 (C) Yes, I would like one.　　(D) I like to do it.

Answer: C、A、A

1 句子的意思是「你想再吃點沙拉嗎？」「不，謝謝。我吃飽了。」
在 Would you like...? 的句型中，like 後面可以接名詞、代名詞，
也可以接不定詞，都表示「你想要……嗎？」根據 I am full. 可
以推斷出對方已經吃飽，不想再吃了，所以選 (C)。

2 句子的意思是「今晚你願意來參加舞會嗎？」「我很願意，但
是我今天太忙了。」Would you like to do...? 這個句型可以表
示禮貌的建議或邀請。根據 but I am too busy today. 可以判斷
出回答者一定是想去的，所以空格中應該填寫肯定的回答方式。
而 I'd like to 是 I would like to go to the party. 的簡略說法，與
問話者的問句是統一的，因此答案選 (A)。

3 句子的意思是：「你想去爬山嗎？」「好啊，什麼時候？」
Would you like to...? 的意思是「你想不想要……？」，並不是
問對方「喜不喜歡」，因此正面回應對方邀請的 (A) 為正確答
案。

How about/What about...?

當我們問別人「跟我一起去怎麼樣？」或「改成星期天怎麼樣？」，我們其實是提出建議，想徵求對方的同意，這時就可以用這個句型了。

 關鍵句型 **點**

❶ 這個句型在口語中的使用頻率很高，意思是「……怎麼樣？」，用來徵求意見、詢問消息或提出建議。多數情況是表達「建議和對方一起做某事」。

❷ What about 和 How about 是可以互換的，表達的意思一樣，都用於表示請求、建議或詢問等。介系詞 about 後面要接名詞或動名詞。

例 **What about** driving to the village?
→開車去那個村莊怎麼樣？
How about Sunday afternoon?
→星期天下午怎麼樣？

會話演練 線

會話翻譯

A **What about** driving to the village?	A: 開車去那個村莊怎麼樣？
B Driving? But it's too far.	B: 開車？但是太遠了。

A Where should we go on vacation?	A: 我們該去哪裡度假呢？
B **How about** Hawaii?	B: 去夏威夷怎麼樣？

A **How about** having dinner with me?	A: 和我一起吃晚餐怎麼樣？
B Sounds great!	B: 聽起來很棒！

A **How about** Sunday afternoon?	A: 星期天下午怎麼樣？
B Sunday afternoon would be fine.	B: 星期天下午沒問題。

A When should we go see the movie?	A：我們該什麼時候去看電影？
B **How about** tomorrow?	B：明天如何？

例句 **一連發**

❶ **What about** that brand of shampoo?
那個牌子的洗髮精怎麼樣？

❷ **What about** another cup of tea?
再來一杯茶怎麼樣？

❸ Here are two skirts you can choose from. **How about** the pink one?
這兩條裙子給你選。那麼那件粉紅色的怎麼樣呢？

❹ **How about** that storm last night?
昨天晚上的暴風雨是怎樣的情況呢？

❺ **What about** going to the cinema with me?
和我去看電影怎麼樣？

❻ **How about** playing chess after school?
放學後下一盤棋怎麼樣？

❼ **What about** that new restaurant?
那家新開的餐廳怎麼樣？

❽ **What about** going together?
一起去怎麼樣？

❾ **How about** singing a song for us?
為我們唱首歌好嗎？

❿ I say, **what about** sending him a copy?
我說，寄一份影本給他怎麼樣？

小小試身手

( ) ❶ –I don't like this blue hat.
　　 –_____ the red one?
　　 (A) What about to buy 　　 (B) Will you buy
　　 (C) Then buy 　　　　　　 (D) How about

( ) ❷ –I have failed five times.
　　 –How about _____ again?
　　 (A) to try 　　　　　　　 (B) trying
　　 (C) tried 　　　　　　　　 (D) try

( ) ❸ How about _____ picnicking next weekend?
　　 (A) go 　　　　　　　　　 (B) going
　　 (C) we will go 　　　　　　 (D) to go

Answer: **D、B、B**

❶ 句子的意思是「我不喜歡這頂藍色帽子。」「那麼這頂紅色的呢？」這裡要注意的是句型 What about/How about 的用法。What about 或 How about 在這裡是說話者詢問對方對某物或某事的看法，意思是「……怎麼樣」。B 和 C 雖然在文法上沒有問題，但是顯得很唐突，因為從對話中可推斷這應該是售貨員在替顧客挑選帽子，顧客對藍色的帽子不喜歡，所以售貨員又詢問顧客對另外一頂紅色帽子的感覺如何。禮貌客氣的詢問意見當然要用 What about/How about...。而介系詞 about 後面要接名詞或動名詞，所以答案是 (D)。

❷ 句子的意思是「我已經失敗五次了。」「再試一次如何？」What about 或 How about 在這裡是用來向對方提出建議，意思是「……怎麼樣？」。介系詞 about 後面要接名詞或動名詞，所以選動名詞 trying，答案是 (B)。

❸ 句子的意思是：「下週末去野餐怎麼樣？」，How about...? 句型中，How about 之後要接 V+ing，因此 (B) 為正確答案。

Unit 06 How long/soon/often...?

當我們想要詢問他人「做⋯⋯需要多久的時間?」或是「過多久以後會做某事?」都可以用到「How long/soon/often...?」這個句型喔!

 關鍵句型 **點**

❶ How long...? 是就時間長短來詢問,詢問某延續性動作會持續「多長的一段時間」。此時,問句裡要使用持續性動詞。回答時用表示一段時間的詞語,如:for three days(三天),since 2008(從 2008 年開始到現在)等。

例 —**How long** have you lived here? →你住在這裡多久了?
　—For three years. →三年了。

❷ How soon...? 通常是用來詢問「過多久以後就做某事?」通常與一般未來式連用。回答時常用「in +時間」。

例 —**How soon** can we see each other again?
　　→我們多久才能再見面?
　—Maybe in one month. →或許一個月後吧!

❸ How often 是針對頻率詢問做某事「多久一次」或「多常做」。回答時常用頻率副詞 often(時常)、sometimes(有時)、usually(通常)、once a week(一星期一次)、twice a month(一個月兩次)等。

例 —**How often** do you visit your parents?
　　→你多久回去探望你的父母一次?
　—Once a week. →一星期一次。

會話演練 **線**

會話翻譯

A **How long** will this boring speech last?

B About 20 minutes.

A: 這個無聊的演講要持續多久？

B: 大概 20 分鐘。

A **How long** have you lived here?

B For three years.

A: 你住在這裡多久了？

B: 3 年了。

A **How soon** can we see each other again?

B Maybe in one month.

A: 我們多久才能再見面？

B: 或許一個月後吧。

A **How often** do you visit your parents?

B Once a week.

A: 你多久回去探望你的父母一次？

B: 一星期一次。

A **How often** do you eat at this restaurant?

B At least once a week.

A：你多久來這家餐廳吃一次？

B：至少一個禮拜一次。

例句**一連發**

❶ How long does it take to fly to Shanghai?
搭飛機到上海需要多長時間？

❷ How long will it take for us to regain our energy by resting?
我們需要休息多長時間才能恢復體力？

❸ How long have you been learning French?
你學法文多久了？

❹ How long is your visit to Taipei?
你會在台北待多長時間？

❺ How soon will you finish your homework?
你要多久才能完成作業？

❻ How soon will you inform me of the result?
你多久後才會通知我結果？

❼ How often do you go home?
你多久回家一次？

❽ How often do you go to see a film?
你多久看一次電影？

❾ How often do you exercise?
你多久運動一次？

小小試身手

( ) ❶ – _____ have the Whites been staying in Paris?
– For three years.
(A) How long　　　　(B) How soon
(C) How far　　　　 (D) How often

( ) ❷ –How often do you go to the library?
–_____.
(A) For three days　　(B) Ten o'clock
(C) Twice a month　　(D) In one month

( ) ❸ –How _____ do we have to wait?
–Just another twenty minutes, I think.
(A) longer　　　　　(B) often
(C) much　　　　　 (D) long

Answer: **A、C、D**

❶ 句子的意思是「懷特一家在巴黎待了多久？」「三年了。」這裡要注意的是句型 How long...? / How soon...? / How far...? / How often... ? 的意義和用法各自不同。首先排除的是 How far...? 因為它是用來詢問距離，而這個題目詢問的是時間，所以不對。(A)、(B)、(D) 三個選項都是詢問時間，但是我們根據現在完成式 have stayed 可以判斷這裡是詢問某延續性動作持續了「多長時間」，所以應該是 How long，答案選 (A)。

❷ 句子的意思是「你多久去圖書館一次？」由於這裡是用 How often 詢問，也就是詢問「去圖書館的頻率」，回答時要說明「多久一次」。只有 (C) 選項 Twice a month（一個月兩次）是針對 How often...? 做出回答。所以答案應該選 (C)。

❸ 句子的意思是：「我們得等多久？」「再二十分鐘吧，我想。」根據回答者的答案，可推測提問的人想知道需要等的時間長度（也就是二十分鐘），因此表示時間長度的 (D) 為正確答案。要是選 (B) 的話就變成了需要等待的頻率，和回答者所說的話不符。

Unit 07 too...+for sb./ sth.+to...

在中文裡，當我們說「這東西太重了，我搬不動」或「這題目太難了，我不會」，英文裡就是要使用這個句型。要注意的是句型中的「to」含有否定意味，就像中文句子裡的「不」。

 關鍵句型

❶ 句型「too... + (for sb./sth.) + to...」表面上看起來是肯定語氣，但其實表達了否定意義，意思是「太……而不能……」或「太……以至於無法……」。too 後面接形容詞或副詞，表示否定的原因；to 後面要接原形動詞，表示否定的內容。而句子當中的 for sb./sth. 則表示「對某人／某事而言」。

例 It's **too dangerous** for you **to cross** the street by yourself. →你自己過馬路太危險了。

❷ 要注意的是，如果在 too...to... 的前面出現了 only，不僅失去了否定意義，反而加強了它的肯定語氣，only too 相當於 very 或 very much。

例 I shall be **only too** pleased **to** come. →我非常樂意來。

❸ 另外，不得不提的是與 too...to 相反的句型，即：too...not to...。因為 not to... 是在原來句型上加了否定詞構成了雙重否定，所以表達的是肯定意義，常可譯成「非常……一定能」或「太……不會不……」。

會話演練 線

會話翻譯

A It's **too** dangerous **for you to** cross the street by yourself.

A: 你自己過馬路太危險了。

B Don't worry, Mom. I'm already 15.

B: 別擔心，媽媽。我已經十五歲了。

A May I help you?

A: 需要我幫忙嗎？

B Well, I'm afraid the luggage is **too** heavy **for you to** carry, but thank you all the same.

B: 不了。這行李太重，恐怕你搬不動。不過還是謝謝你。

A Why didn't you ask for her signature?

A: 你為什麼沒有要她的簽名？

B Oh, I was **too** excited **to** remember to do that.

B: 噢！我太興奮以至於忘了這件事。

A Please come visit my farm if you are free.

A: 如果你有空的話，請來我的農場。

B I shall be **only too** pleased **to** come.

B: 我非常樂意。

例句**一連發**

❶ He is **too** young **to** join the army.
他年紀太小，不能加入軍隊。

❷ The bridge is **too** narrow **for five people to** pass.
這座橋太窄了，沒辦法讓五個人同時過。

❸ I went **too** late **to** get a ticket.
我太晚去了，沒有買到票。

❹ The math problem is **too** difficult **for her to** work out.
這道數學題目太難，她解不出來。

❺ One is **never too** old **to** learn.
活到老，學到老。

❻ I'm **not too** old **to** climb the mountain with you.
我還不算太老，仍可以和你們一起去爬山。

❼ I'm **only too** pleased **to** be able to help you.
我非常高興能幫助你。

小小試身手

( ) ❶ Can you tell me what the teacher wrote on the blackboard? My eyesight is _____ poor for me _____ read such small letters.
(A) so / that
(B) so / as to
(C) too / to
(D) enough / to

( ) ❷ These fans are _____ eager _____ their idols.
(A) so / that see
(B) so / that they don't want to see
(C) not too / to see
(D) too / to see

Answer: C、D

❶ 句子的意思是「你能告訴我老師在黑板上寫了什麼嗎？我的視力太差，看不清楚那麼小的字。」這裡要注意的是句型 too...to... 和 so...that..., so as to, enough...to... 的用法不同。因為 so...that... 句型要求 that 後面接完整句子，而 read such small letters 不是完整的句子，所以首先排除 A。A,B,D 選項都表示「太……以至於可以……」、「太……所以能……」等肯定涵義，所以不符合題意。題目中要求的是否定內容 read such small letters，所以選 too...to 表示「太……而不能……」，答案是 (C)。

❷ 句子的意思是「這些粉絲太急於想要見到他們的偶像了。」so...that... 後面要接完整句子，所以排除 (A)；(B) 選項的 that 後面雖然接了完整句子，但表達的意思是「不想見到偶像」，顯然不符合句子的意思；(C) 選項的 not too...to... 表示肯定意義，有「會／能做……」、「不太……，能夠……」的意思，也不符合句子的意思。要注意的是，原本 too...to 的句型中表達了否定意涵，但是當 too...to 句型中的 too 後面接的是表示情緒的形容詞如 eager, glad, sad 等時，則表示肯定意義，即「太……，能夠……」，所以符合題意，故正確選項為 (D)。

Unit 08 (not) + ... + enough + (...) + to do sth.

中文裡的「夠不夠」，就是用這個句型來表達，例如：「這些食物夠不夠我們吃？」或「我們有足夠的時間讓我們完成這件事。」

關鍵句型 **點**

❶ 在「... + enough（ + ...）+ to do sth.」這個句型中，enough 意為「足夠的」，表示剛好達到某種程度、數量等。enough 可以修飾形容詞、副詞和名詞。enough 作形容詞時，用來修飾名詞，可以放在名詞前面，也可以放在名詞後面；enough 作副詞時，可以放在所修飾的形容詞或副詞後面。

例 Do you have **enough** money **to** buy a computer?
　　→你有足夠的錢買電腦嗎？

❷ 句型「not + ... + enough（ + ...）+ to do sth.」是這個句型的否定形式。

例 My son did **not** do well **enough to** pass the final exams.
　　→我兒子考得不好，期末考試沒通過。

❸ 另外，「... + enough（ +名詞）+ (for +名詞 / 代名詞) + to do sth.」句型中有時會出現「for +名詞 / 代名詞」，表示「對……而言」。

例 Please write clearly **enough for me to** read next time.
　　→下次請寫清楚，好讓我看懂。

會話演練 線

會話翻譯

(not) + ... + enough + (...) + to do sth.

A Do you have **enough** money **to** buy a computer?

B Yes. I have been saving some money for buying a computer these two years.

A: 你有足夠的錢買電腦嗎？

B: 有的，這兩年我為了買電腦存了一些錢。

A What are you bothered about?

B My son did **not** do well **enough to** pass the final exams.

A: 你為什麼煩心呢？

B: 我兒子考得不好，期末考試沒通過。

A Please write clearly **enough for me to** read next time.

B Ok. Let me write it again now.

A: 請你下次寫清楚，好讓我看懂。

B: 好的，我現在就重寫一遍吧。

A Everyone is thirsty.

B But there **aren't enough** drinks **for** everyone.

A: 每個人都渴了。

B: 但是飲料不夠分給每個人。

例句 **一連發**

❶ The closet is big **enough for** you **to** hide in.
這衣櫃大得可以讓你藏進去。

❷ There is **enough** food **for** all of us.
食物足夠我們所有人吃。

❸ You are old **enough to** take good care of yourself now.
你現在夠大了，可以照顧好自己。

❹ I have **enough** time **to** get to the railway station.
我有足夠的時間趕到火車站。

❺ She is not old **enough to** get married.
她還不到可以結婚的年紀。

❻ Tom didn't run fast **enough to** catch the early bus.
湯姆跑得不夠快，沒趕上早班巴士。

❼ They were standing near **enough for** us **to** overhear their conversation.
他們站得離我們太近了，我們都能聽見他們的談話。

❽ We have **enough** seats **for** everyone.
我們有足夠的座位提供給每個人坐。

小小 **試身手**

( ) ❶ He was _____ to understand the teacher's questions.
(A) quick enough   (B) enough quick
(C) quick as   (D) such quick

( ) ❷ The bookstore did not prepare _____ books for all students in the class.
(A) plenty of   (B) enough
(C) enough of   (D) as many

( ) ❸ There isn't _____ all the cats.
(A) milk enough to   (B) enough milk to
(C) milk enough for   (D) enough milk for

Answer: **A、B、D**

❶ 句子的意思是「他反應很快，可以理解老師的問題。」在這個句子中，enough 用來修飾形容詞 quick，要放在 quick 的後面，即 quick enough，因此答案選 (A)。

❷ 句子的意思是「書店沒有準備足夠的書給班上所有的學生。」plenty of 不能用在否定句中。而根據句中否定形式 did not 可以判斷題目想要表達的最恰當含義是「書的數量不夠多，所以不是班上所有的學生都有書」。所以答案為 (B)。

❸ 句子的意思是：「沒有足夠的牛奶給全部的貓。」由於 all the cats 為名詞片語，前面不適合接 enough... to... 句型，可先刪除前兩項。「be enough N for...」為正確的排列順序，所以 (D) 為正確答案。

Let's/Let us...

中文裡所說的「讓我們把這件事完成吧！」或「我們走吧！」，在英文裡就是用這個句型，但 Let's 和 Let us 的意思並不完全相同哦！讓我們來看看是哪裡不同吧！

 關鍵句型 **點**

❶ 這是祈使句的常用句型。Let's和Let us都有「讓我們……」的意思，句首的let意思是「讓」，後面要接原形動詞。但是Let's和Let us仍然有些不同：Let's説的「我們」包括説者自己和聽者。所以，它的附加問句就應該是shall we，即：Let's..., shall we?

例 Susan, **let's** go for a drive somewhere this Saturday, shall we?
　→蘇珊，這星期六讓我們開車去某個地方兜風吧？

Let us 説的「我們」不包括聽者在內，只是説者向聽者提出請求或建議等。所以，它的附加問句就應該是 will you，即：Let us..., will you?

例 **Let us** go home, will you? →讓我們回家吧，可以嗎？

會話演練 線

會話翻譯

A Susan, **let's** go for a drive somewhere this Saturday.	A: 蘇珊，這星期六讓我們開車去某個地方兜風吧？
B That's a good idea. Just the two of us!	B: 真是好主意。就我們兩個去吧！

A I feel kind of blue today.	A: 我今天有點鬱悶。
B **Let's** go for a walk.	B: 讓我們去散散步吧。

A **Let's** go to the concert, shall we?	A: 讓我們去聽音樂會吧，怎麼樣？
B Sorry. I must wait for my friend at home.	B: 對不起，我必須在家等朋友。

A Go and send these invitation cards to our guests.	A: 去把這些邀請卡發送給我們的客人。
B But it's too late. **Let us** go home, will you?	B: 但是太晚了，讓我們回家吧，可以嗎？

A Please **let us** go!	A: 請讓我們走吧！
B Not until you give me all your money.	B: 先把你們的錢通通給我。

例句 **一連發**

❶ Tomorrow is Christmas. **Let's** have a party.
明天是聖誕節，我們來舉辦派對吧！

❷ **Let's** go to the beach for the vacation.
讓我們去海邊度個假吧！

❸ —**Let's** go dancing tonight!
—Sounds great!
一今天晚上去跳舞吧！
一好主意！

❹ **Let us** wait for you in the reading-room, will you?
我們在閱覽室等你，好嗎？

❺ **Let us** go shopping, will you?
讓我們去購物，好嗎？

❻ **Let's** get there at about six o'clock, shall we?
我們六點鐘左右到那裡，好嗎？

❼ **Let's** not talk about it anymore.
我們不要再談論此事了。

小小**試身手**

( ) ❶ _____ go hunting, will you?
    (A) Let's to   (B) Let's
    (C) Let us   (D) Let us to

( ) ❷ Let's try a bit harder, _____?
    (A) will we   (B) shall we
    (C) do we   (D) are we

( ) ❸ – _____ go swimming!
    – We can't, our parents will never _____.
    (A) Let us / let's   (B) Let's / let's
    (C) Let me / let us   (D) Let's / let us

Answer: **C、B、D**

❶ 句子的意思是「讓我們去打獵，好嗎？」因為 let 後面要用原形
動詞，所以首先排除 (A)、(D)；其次，根據題目中的附加問句
是 will you，可以得知這句話是在向聽者提出打獵的請求，希望
聽者能答應。聽者並不參與打獵活動本身，所以句子前半部要
用 Let us，因此答案是 (C)。

❷ 句子的意思是「讓我們再努力一點，好嗎？」因為句子前半部
是 Let's，這説明了説者提出的請求和建議是針對聽者，聽者也
參與其中，換句話説，説者和聽者雙方都參與這個建議內容，
因此附加問句要用 shall we，答案選 (B)。

❸ 句子的意思是：「我們去游泳吧！」「不行啦，我們的父母不
會讓我們去的。」第一句為表達邀約兩人一起去，而非尋求答
者的允許，因此選擇 Let's；而第二句中答者提到的是父母不會
「允許」，需選擇 let us，因此 (D) 為正確答案。

Unit 10

get + V-ed...

在中文裡，我們如果瞬間有了某種感覺或做了某件事，強調在某個時間突然發生，就是用這個句型，例如：I got hurt.（我受傷了）跟 I am hurt. 其實很像，只是 I got hurt. 強調突然受傷了，而 I am hurt. 強調受傷的狀態。

 關鍵句型 **點**

❶ 句型「get + V-ed」主要是口語表達，可以用來代替「be 動詞 + V-ed」，構成被動結構。此時，常表示一種突發性的事件、遭遇，或用於談論設法或終於做到令人稱心的事，帶有較強烈的感情色彩。

例 He **got hurt** when he was biking to school.
　　→他在騎車上學的途中受傷了。

❷ get 與過去分詞連用時，常表示狀態（包括情感）的變化和動作的結果，get 表示一種狀態向另一種狀態過渡、變化的動作，後面一般不接「by ＋主動者」。

例 I got confused at what you said.
　　→我被你說的話搞糊塗了。

會話演練 **線**

會話翻譯

A Do you understand?	A: 明白了嗎？
B Sorry, I **got confused** at what you said.	B: 抱歉，我被你説的話搞糊塗了。

A When did they **get engaged**?	A: 他們什麼時候訂婚的？
B Last month.	B: 上個月。

A I **got surprised** at the news.	A: 這個消息真令我驚訝。
B So did I.	B: 我也是。

A What happened to your son?	A: 你的兒子怎麼了？
B He **got hurt** when he was biking to school.	B: 他在騎車上學的途中受傷了。

A What took you so long?	A: 你怎麼遲到那麼久？
B Sorry, I **got lost** on the way.	B: 抱歉，我在路上迷路了。

例句 **一連發**

❶ The little girl **got lost** in the forest.
小女孩在森林裡迷了路。

❷ He went out and **got drunk** yesterday evening.
昨天傍晚他出去並且喝醉了。

❸ Five soldiers **got wounded** in the battle.
五個士兵在那場戰爭中受了傷。

❹ Don't **get caught** in the storm!
別被暴風雨困住了！

❺ I nearly **got hit** by the car just now.
我剛才差一點被那輛車撞到。

❻ He **got dumped** by Jenny last week.
他上個星期被珍妮甩了。

❼ Many tourists **got killed** in this country last month.
許多觀光客上個月在這個國家遇害。

小小試身手

( ) ❶ Soon the square became ____.
    (A) crowded many people
    (B) crowds
    (C) crowding
    (D) crowded

( ) ❷ I don't like sports in which people easily ____.
    (A) get hurt   (B) got hurt
    (C) got hurted   (D) get

( ) ❸ Don't have too much beer! You could get _____.
    (A) hurt   (B) drunk
    (C) wounded   (D) hit

Answer: **D、A、B**

❶ 這句的意思是「很快地廣場上就擠滿了人」。這裡使用的句型是 become + V-ed。become 在這裡的用法和 get + V-ed 一樣，後面要接過去分詞。四個選項中只有 crowded 符合句型要求。become crowded 用來強調主詞 the square（廣場）慢慢擁擠的狀態變化，因此答案選 (D)。

❷ 句子的意思是「我不喜歡容易使人受傷的運動」。這裡使用的句型是 get + V-ed。get hurt 是一種習慣說法，表示人受傷的狀態。hurt 的過去分詞仍然是 hurt，所以正確選項為 (A)。

❸ 句子的意思是：「不要喝那麼多酒！你會醉的。」可以推測，喝了太多啤酒後最有可能發生的情況是 (B) 所敘述的喝醉，(A) 和 (C) 中所提及的受傷和 (D) 中提及的被打較無直接關聯，故答案要選 (B)。

Unit 11

Once...

中文裡的「一旦……」例如：「一旦你招認，你就會被送進大牢」或「一旦你答應了，你就必須遵守諾言」，就是使用這個句型。

 關鍵句型 **點**

❶ 「once ＋時間子句＋主句」，意思是「一旦……就……」、「一……就……」。這個句型表示時間上的兩個動作或兩件事彼此緊接著發生，且含有條件意味。

例 Once you begin, you must go on.
→你一旦開了頭，就必須繼續下去。

❷ 若時間子句中的主詞與主句的主詞相同，且主詞中含有 be 時，可以省略子句的主詞和 be。

例 Once printed, your novel will be very popular.
→一旦出版，你這本小說就會很暢銷。

以上這個例句的完整寫法應為：

Once your novel is printed, your novel will be very popular.

會話演練 **線**

會話翻譯

A I want to give it up.

B **Once** you begin, you must go on.

A: 我想放棄了。

B: 你一旦開了頭，就必須繼續下去。

A **Once** we have passed the exam, we will be able to relax.

B Come on! Let's relax right now.

A: 一旦通過了考試，我們就可以輕鬆一下。

B: 拜託，我們現在就放鬆一下吧！

A I'm not confident of my novel at all.

B Don't worry. **Once** printed, your novel will be very popular.

A: 我對我的小說一點信心都沒有。

B: 別擔心。一旦出版，這本小說一定會很暢銷。

A Are you sure this makeup style looks good on me?

B **Once** I finish, you'll see how great you look!

A: 你確定這個妝容適合我嗎？

B: 我一化完以後，你就會看到有多好看了。

例句 **一連發**

❶ Once my brother began to play online games, he couldn't stop.
一旦我弟弟開始玩線上遊戲,他就停不下來。

❷ Once heated, the amber can be made into any shape.
琥珀一旦加熱,就可以被製作成各種形狀。

❸ Once you see him, you will never forget him.
一旦你看見他,就再也忘不了他。

❹ Once (it is) found, any mistake must be corrected.
一旦發現任何錯誤,就必須加以改正。

❺ Once you understand the rules of the game, you will enjoy it.
一旦瞭解了遊戲規則,你就會喜歡上這個遊戲。

❻ Once you make a promise, you should keep it.
你一旦許下諾言,就應該遵守。

❼ Once you grow up, you will understand all these things.
一旦你長大,你就會了解這些所有的事。

小小試身手

( ) ❶ ____ you lose it, you lose it forever.
(A) when　　　　(B) Suddenly
(C) Once　　　　(D) Even if

( ) ❷ ____ environmental damage is done, it takes many years for the ecosystem to recover.
(A) Even if　　　(B) If only
(C) While　　　　(D) Once

( ) ❸ Once _____, you must let me know right away.
(A) found　　　　(B) you found
(C) find it　　　　(D) you find it

Answer: C、D、D

❶ 這句的意思是「你一旦失去了它，你就會永遠失去它。」根據句子的意思，首先可以排除 D，因為 even if 表示「即使」；而 suddenly 不能引導子句，所以排除 (B)。這個句子中的子句含有條件關係，即子句是主句的條件，所以排除 (A)，最佳答案應該是 (C)。

❷ 這句的意思是「環境一旦被破壞，要想修復生態系統就需要花很多年的時間。」even if 的意思是「即使」，if only 的意思是「只要」，while 意思是「當……」，意思和邏輯關係都不符合句意，只有 once 表示「一旦……就……」能說明子句是主句的條件，所以正確答案是 (D)。

❸ 句子的意思是：「一旦你找到它，請立刻讓我知道。」只看前半句的話，此句型結構只可選擇 (A) 或 (D)，然而後半句的主詞為 you，而 you 不是要「find」（找到）的對象，因為說話者現在就已經在跟他講話，根本沒有需要尋找他。需要被找的應該是「it」，因此選擇 (D) 為正確答案。

Level 1 過關大挑戰

❶ ____lots of children on the square.
(A) There is   (B) We have
(C) There are   (D) It has

❷ ____ice and water all over the forest after the heavy snow.
(A) It has   (B) There is
(C) There are   (D) They are

❸ A: Would you please lend some money to me?
   B: ____. Here you are.
(A) Yes, I would   (B) No, I wouldn't
(C) Certainly   (D) No, I'm sorry

❹ A: What's the climate ____ there?
   B: It's very pleasant.
(A) X   (B) like
(C) look like   (D) look

❺ Let's have a party, ____ ?
(A) will you   (B) shall we
(C) will we   (D) have we

❻ Would you like ____ some juice? ____.
(A) X / Yes, I'd like some coffee   (B) X / No, please not
(C) have / Yes, thanks   (D) to have / No, thanks

7 How about _____ with me?
- (A) to go traveling
- (B) to go to traveling
- (C) going traveling
- (D) go to travel

8 _____ will the meeting last?
- (A) How long
- (B) How often
- (C) When
- (D) How soon

9 A: _____ will she come back from abroad?
B: In three months.
- (A) How soon
- (B) How often
- (C) How long
- (D) When

10 Your idea sounds _____, but what should we do first?
- (A) bad
- (B) badly
- (C) good
- (D) well

11 She was _____ excited to _____ all night long.
- (A) so / wake
- (B) so / sleep
- (C) too / wake
- (D) too / sleep

12 _____ everything _____ perfect.
- (A) Not / is
- (B) Not / are
- (C) No / is
- (D) X / aren't

13 I haven't got _____ _____ you.
- (A) enough breads / to
- (B) enough breads / for
- (C) bread enough / to
- (D) bread enough / for

14 There _____ enough teachers _____ so many students.
- (A) is / for teach
- (B) is / to teach
- (C) are / to teach
- (D) are / for teaching

❶ There be 句型表示「某地有某物／某人」。be 動詞要與主詞的單複數一致，而主詞 children 是可數名詞 child 的複數形式，所以 be 動詞要用 are，答案選 (C)。

❷ 首先確認要用 There be 句型。其次，這裡的主詞有兩個，分別是 ice 和 water，而 be 動詞要遵循「就近原則」，所以根據不可數名詞 ice，可知 be 動詞要用 is，所以選 (B)。

❸ Would you please...? 這個句型用於向某人提出詢問、請求，意思是「你可以……嗎？」或「可不可以請你……？」。Would 在這裡並不表示過去時態，而表示更加委婉和客氣的請求。回答這個句型時，如果願意，可以說 Yes, I'll be glad to. / Certainly. / Of course. 等；如果不願意或不能夠，可以說 No, I'm sorry. / Sorry, but... 等。但根據後面的 Here you are（給你）可以判斷，回答者是願意借錢給對方的，所以應該用 Certainly「當然可以」，選 (C)。

❹ What is ...like? 這個句型常可以用來詢問天氣、氣候。What is ＋名詞 ...? 則是用來詢問某物「是什麼」或某人的職業、職務或社會地位等「是什麼」。look like 放在 what 疑問句中前面要用助動詞 does，即 What does...look like?，因此答案為 (B)。

❺ 當句子前半部是 Let's 時，表示說者提出的請求和建議也是針對聽者的，聽者也參與其中。換句話說，說者和聽者雙方都參與這個建議內容，因此附加問句要用 shall we，答案選 (B)。

❻ 句型 Would you like...? 表示「你想要……嗎？」，用來表示禮貌的請求、建議，或詢問對方是否需要什麼，或徵求意見與看法。like 後面可以接名詞或代名詞，也可以接不定詞。但是在回答時，如果是肯定，就用 Yes, please；如果是否定的，就用 No, thanks.，所以選 (D)。

❼ How about...? 用來徵求意見、詢問消息或提出建議，意思是「……怎麼樣？」在這個句型中，介系詞 about 後面不能接不定詞或原形動詞，而要接名詞或動名詞。所以後面的 go 要改成動名詞形式 going traveling。所以選 (C)。

❽ 這裡要注意的是句型 How long...? / When...? / How soon...? / How often... ? 之間的不同。用 How often 是詢問「多久做某事一次？」；When 是詢問「什麼時候？」；How soon 表示從現在起的「多久以後？」；這三個選項都不符

合題意「這個會議要持續多久？」；只有 How long 是詢問做某事或某個動作的時間長短，意思是「多長時間／多久」，所以選 (A)。

9 這句問的是「她多久以後從國外回來？」回答是「三個月後。」也就是從現在起算三個月後，所以必須選 How soon（多久以後），答案是 (A)。

10 本題的 sound 是典型的感官動詞，此時它的後面可以接形容詞。而從 but what should we do first？（但是我們應該先做什麼？）說明已經肯定了這個想法是好的，所以不能選 bad，答案是 (C)。

11 句型 too...to... 是肯定形式表達否定意義，意思是「太……而不能……」或「太……以至於無法……」，too 後面接形容詞或副詞，表示否定的原因；to 後面接原形動詞表示否定的內容。正常邏輯應該是因為她 too excited，所以導致整夜無法入睡，所以 to 後應該接 sleep。正確答案是 (D)。這個句子相當於 She was so excited that she couldn't sleep all night long.

12 在英語中，all, both, every 等與 not 連用，構成部分否定，意思是「並非……都……」。everything 後面的動詞要用單數，所以選 (A)，句子的意思是「並非一切都是完美的。」

13 句型「... + enough + for +名詞 / 代名詞」意思是「……對……是足夠的」。enough 作形容詞時，意思是「足夠的」，可以修飾名詞。此時，既可放在名詞前，也可以放在名詞後。bread 是不可數名詞，不能寫成 breads，所以正確答案是 (D)。

14 there be 句型中的 be 動詞要與後面的 enough teachers 保持單複數的一致，teachers 是複數可數名詞，所以 be 動詞要用 are。enough 在這裡修飾名詞 teachers，後面接不定詞 to do sth.，所以正確答案是 (C)。

過關測驗解答

01~05: (C) (B) (C) (B) (B)　　　　　11~14: (D) (A) (D) (C)
06~10: (D) (C) (A) (A) (C)

Level 1
補充文法面

瞭解 5 種主要詞性，破解 5 大基本句型

英文句型與英文文法的關係密不可分，所以在開始學習句型之前，我們先來複習幾個簡單的文法概念，這些文法概念可以幫助你學習句型，很快的掌握學習重點。首先，我們先來瞭解英文文法的詞性，最主要的詞性可以分為：

1▷名詞

在英文裡，名詞可以分為可數名詞和不可數名詞，例如一顆一顆數得出來的蘋果（apple）就是可數，而像水（water）這樣的東西就是不可數名詞。另外，針對可數名詞來說，又可以分為單數名詞和複數名詞，如前面所講的蘋果（apple），它的單數就是 apple，複數就是 apples。

2▷代名詞

代名詞顧名思義就是代替名詞的詞，也就是説，當我們不想説出名詞時，就可以用代名詞代替，例如剛剛所提到的名詞 apple，單數 apple 的代名詞就是 it，而複數 apples 的代名詞就是 they。

3▷動詞

動詞可説是一個句子當中的靈魂人物，它可以幫助句子動起來，例如：run（跑）、fly（飛）、eat（吃）……等描述動作的單字都算是動詞。另外還有一種所謂的 be 動詞，中文通常翻譯成「是」，例如 am、are、is 等都是。

4 形容詞

在一個句子當中，形容詞所扮演的角色其實是用來襯托名詞的，如果名詞是主角，形容詞就是配角；如果名詞是新娘，形容詞就是伴娘。再以剛剛所提到的 apple 來解釋，apple 是名詞，而 red（紅色的）就是用來形容 apple 的形容詞，即 a red apple（一顆紅色的蘋果）。

5 副詞

副詞在句子當中所扮演的是修飾動詞的角色，例如剛剛所說的動詞 run（跑）、fly（飛），如果我們要進一步修飾動詞，我們可以說「跑得快」（run fast）、「飛得高」（fly high），fast 和 high 都是所謂的副詞。

瞭解名詞、代名詞、動詞、形容詞、副詞這五個主要的詞性之後，我們就要開始進入句型的主題了。雖然英文句型看起來既多又複雜，但其實我們最常用的句型不外乎下列五種：

❶ S ＋ V   ❹ S ＋ V ＋ O ＋ O
❷ S ＋ V ＋ SC   ❺ S ＋ V ＋ O ＋ OC
❸ S ＋ V ＋ O

看到上面密密麻麻的英文字你一定嚇壞了，不用擔心，接下來我們會一一介紹每個句型中，英文字母所代表的含意，看完我們的解說後，你就會發現一點都不難。

1. S（主詞）：

主詞是句子當中「做出動作」的人或物，例如：在 Birds fly.（鳥飛）這個句子中，我們先找出動詞 fly（飛），然後再看看是誰在飛，發現是 Birds 在飛，所以 Birds 就是這個句子當中的主詞。

2. V（動詞）：

剛剛所提到的 Birds fly.（鳥飛）這個句子中，很明顯的，fly（飛）就是動詞，也就是句子當中表現出動作的字。

3. O（受詞）：

受詞就是「承受動作的物件」，例如：I eat apple.（我吃蘋果）這個句子中，我們先找出動詞是 eat（吃），然後找出是 I（我）在吃，所以 I 是主詞，接下來就找出是誰被吃，發現是 apple（蘋果）被吃，apple 承受了「吃」的這個動作，所以是受詞。

4. C（補語）：

補語顧名思義就是用來「補充說明」的字，例如：I am a student.（我是學生）這個句子中，先找出動詞是 am（Be 動詞），然後找出主詞是 I，但是只有 I am（我是）並不能構成完整句子，也就是說句子意義不明確，所以我們在後面加上補語 a student，就構成完整句子了。另外，補語又可以分成主詞補語和受詞補語，剛剛所提到的 I am a student. 句子當中，a student 是用來補充主詞 I 的不足，也就是針對主詞 I 加以補充說明，所以是主詞補語（SC）。

因此，受詞補語（OC）就是針對受詞加以補充說明的單字，例如：I made her cry.（我使她哭了）這個句子中，先找出動詞是 made（使），然後是主詞 I，受詞 her，但是只有 I made her（我使她）的句子是不完整的，所以我們在後面加了受詞補語 cry（哭），也就是說，是「她哭了」，而不是「我哭了」，所以 cry 是用來修飾受詞 her，而不是用來修飾主詞 I，所以這個句子當中的 cry 是受詞補語。

瞭解了主詞、動詞、受詞、補語這四個句子的主要組成成分後，我們就可以回過頭來看看前面所提到的五大基本句型了：

❶ S + V   ❹ S + V + O + O
❷ S + V + SC   ❺ S + V + O + OC
❸ S + V + O

再重新看這五個句型，你是不是覺得很簡單了呢？

首先，第一個句型 **S + V** 就是「主詞＋動詞」，也就是我們剛剛所說的 Birds fly.（鳥飛）這樣的句型。

第二個句型 **S + V + SC** 就是「主詞＋動詞＋主詞補語」，也就是前面所提的 I am a student.（我是學生）這個句型。

第三個句型 **S + V + O** 就是「主詞＋動詞＋受詞」，也就是之前所講的 I eat apple.（我吃蘋果）這個句型。

第四個句型 **S + V + O + O** 就是「主詞＋動詞＋受詞＋受詞」，在這個句子當中有兩個受詞，較為特殊，舉例來說，I bought a book for him.（我買了一本書給他）這個句子當中，主詞是 I（我），動詞是 bought（買），而 a book 和 him 都是「承受動作的物件」，也就是說，和 bought（買）這個動作都有關係，所以它們兩個都是受詞，這個句子也可以改寫成 I bought him a book.（我買了一本書給他）。

最後，**S + V + O + OC** 就是「主詞＋動詞＋受詞＋受詞補語」，也就是 I made her cry.（我害她哭了。）這個句型。

Level 2

Unit 01 What's the matter (with)...?

在中文裡，當我們說「你怎麼了？」或「你的臉怎麼了？」，我們可能是發現了某些異狀，所以想表達自己的關心，這時就可以用這個句型。

 關鍵句型 **點**

❶ What's the matter (with)...?」是個實用句型，意思是「……怎麼了？」、「……出什麼毛病了？」，這個句型常用來表達對對方的關心，或詢問瞭解一些事物或狀況，而且很多時候，問話者在提問之前多多少少發現和察覺出對方或某事物的不正常情況。在這句型中，matter的意思是「麻煩事」、「問題」、「毛病」；the matter在意義和用法上相當於形容詞wrong。

❷ What's the matter?可以單獨使用，詢問發生了什麼事，意思是「怎麼啦？」相當於What's wrong?或Something wrong?或Tell me what's wrong.。

例 —**What's the matter?** →怎麼啦？
　　—I lost my favorite ring. →我把我最喜歡的戒指弄丟了。

❸ 要特別提及某人或某事物怎麼了時，則要在matter後面加上介系詞with，引出某人或某事物。

例 **What's the matter with** your foot? →你的腳怎麼了？

❹ 在回答這個句型時，經常用anything/something/nothing與matter連用。

例 —**What's the matter with** your computer? →你的電腦怎麼了？
　　—Nothing is the matter. →沒什麼問題。

會話演練 線

會話翻譯

A **What's the matter?**

B I lost my favorite ring.

A: 怎麼啦?

B: 我把我最喜歡的戒指弄丟了。

A **What's the matter?** Why are you crying?

B The movie is too touching.

A: 怎麼啦?你為什麼哭?

B: 這部電影太感人了。

A **What's the matter with** your foot?

B I twisted my left foot yesterday.

A: 你的腳怎麼了?

B: 我昨天扭傷了我的左腳。

A **What's the matter with** your computer?

B Nothing is the matter.

A: 你的電腦怎麼了?

B: 沒有什麼問題。

A **What's the matter with** you today?

B I don't know. I can't concentrate.

A: 你今天是怎麼了?

B: 不知道,我就是專心不下來。

例句**一連發**

❶ What's the matter with you?
你怎麼啦？

❷ What's the matter with your cat?
你的貓怎麼啦？

❸ She didn't attend the meeting. **What's the matter**?
她沒出席會議。出了什麼事？

❹ What's the matter with the car?
車子出了什麼問題？

❺ What's the matter with my lungs, Doctor?
醫生，我的肺出了什麼問題？

❻ Can you tell me **what's the matter with** the project?
你能告訴我這個方案出了什麼問題嗎？

❼ No one knows **what's the matter with** the boss.
沒有人知道老闆怎麼了。

小小試身手

( )❶ What's the matter _____ the television?
(A) to   (B) in
(C) of   (D) with

( )❷ –Can you tell me _____ with the watch?
–It's broken.
(A) what's the matter   (B) what the matter is
(C) what's the wrong   (D) what the wrong is

( )❸ –What's the matter?
–_____
(A) The matter is over here.
(B) I don't know what a matter is.
(C) Nothing, I'm just tired.
(D) That's mine, what's yours?

Answer: **D、A、C**

❶ 句子意思是「這台電視出了什麼問題？」這是句型What's the matter with...?的用法。要詢問某人或某事物怎麼了，要在 What's the matter後面加上介系詞with，引出某人或某事物。所以答案是with，選(D)。

❷ 句子意思是「你能告訴我這支手錶怎麼了嗎？」「它壞了。」 What's the matter with...?和What's wrong with...?都可以用來詢問某人或某物怎麼了，出了什麼毛病等。而因為本題的 What's the matter with my watch在句中是tell的受詞，受詞子句的主詞正好是疑問詞what，因此在受詞子句中不用改變語序，答案為(A)。

❸ 句子的意思是：「怎麼了？」「沒事，我有點累而已。」只要知道 What's the matter 的意思，應該就不會誤解問者想表達的事情而錯選其他選項。正確答案為 (C)。

Unit 02 It doesn't matter (if/whether)...

我們常說的「沒關係」,「你去不去都沒關係」或「就算下雨也沒關係」等,就是用這個句型來表達。

 關鍵句型 **點**

❶ 「It does not matter if/whether...」是一個很有用的句型,意思是「如果……也沒關係。」、「不論(是否)……都沒關係……。」matter在本句型中是當作動詞,意思是「有關係、要緊」。這個句型沒有時態的區別,即不管後面句子是什麼時態,前面都用doesn't matter。

例 **It doesn't matter if** we miss the train, because there's another one later. →我們要是錯過這班火車也不要緊,因為晚一點還有另一班車。

❷ It doesn't matter後面也能接what或how等引導的子句。

例 **It doesn't matter how** you're dressed.
→你不管怎麼穿都沒關係。

❸ It doesn't matter.也可單獨使用。是一個非常實用的口語句型,常用於當別人表示歉意時我們所做出的禮貌回答,意思為「沒關係」、「沒問題」。其他用法相同的句子還有That's OK./That's all right.,值得注意的是,It doesn't matter.不能用來回答Thanks.或Thank you.等,而That's all right.則可以。

例 —I'm sorry; I forgot to bring the copy of our contract.
→很抱歉,我忘了帶合約副本。
—**It doesn't matter.** →沒關係。

會話翻譯

It doesn't matter (if/whether)...

A Quickly! We will miss the train.

B Don't worry. **It doesn't matter if** we miss the train, because there's another one later.

A: 快一點！我們要錯過火車了。

B: 別擔心。我們要是錯過這班火車也沒關係，因為晚一點還有另一班車。

A I have no formal evening dress for the party.

B **It doesn't matter how** you're dressed.

A: 我沒有可以穿去參加晚會的正式晚禮服。

B: 你不管怎麼穿都沒關係。

A Would you like to go and sing karaoke?

B I can't sing well.

A **It doesn't matter.**

A: 你想去唱卡拉 OK 嗎？

B: 我不太會唱歌。

A: 沒關係。

A I'm sorry; I forgot to bring the copy of our contract.

B **It doesn't matter.**

A: 很抱歉，我忘了帶合約副本。

B: 沒關係。

例句**一連發**

❶ **It doesn't matter if** you really can't come.
你真的不能來的話也沒關係。

❷ **It doesn't matter if** you have made mistakes. Learn from your mistakes and you'll make progress.
如果你犯錯了也沒關係。從錯誤中學習，你就會進步。

❸ **It doesn't matter whether** we start now or later.
我們現在開始，還是晚一點開始都沒關係。

❹ **It doesn't matter** to me **if** she tells me the truth.
她是否告訴我事實真相對我來說並不重要。

❺ If a person does his best, **it doesn't matter what** people think of him.
只要一個人盡了力，不管人們怎樣看待都沒關係。

❻ **It doesn't matter whether** he helps us.
他幫不幫我們都沒關係。

❼ **It doesn't matter whether** the weather will be fine tomorrow.
明天天氣好不好都沒關係。

小小試身手

( ) ❶ It _____ matter _____ me which one you choose.
(A) isn't / with　　　(B) doesn't / for
(C) doesn't / to　　　(D) isn't / to

( ) ❷ –I'm afraid I can't get there on time.
　　–_____. We'll wait for you.
(A) It's too bad　　　(B) No problem
(C) All right　　　　(D) It doesn't matter

( ) ❸ It doesn't matter whether you're late or not. _____.
(A) We've got everything under control.
(B) You must be late.
(C) If only you could have come earlier.
(D) Please come on time.

Answer: C、D、A

❶ 句子意思是「對我來說你選擇哪一個都沒關係。」It doesn't matter是固定說法，意思是「沒關係。」It doesn't matter可以單獨使用，也可以在後面接子句，這裡就是which引導的子句。而要進一步表示對誰來說沒關係，則可以在It doesn't matter後面接介系詞to引出sb.。因此答案為(C)。

❷ 句子意思是「我恐怕不能準時到那裡。」「沒關係，我們會等你的。」根據We'll wait for you.可判斷回答者不介意說話者也許會遲到的狀況，所以首先排除(A)。No problem是「沒問題」的意思，常用於別人向你提出幫忙或其他請求時；All right是「好的」的意思，也是答應某人時的回答語；It doesn't matter是「沒關係。」的意思，最符合上下文意思，所以選(D)。

❸ 句子的意思是：「你遲到或沒遲到都沒關係，一切都在我們的掌控之中」。(A) 為正確答案，其他三個選項意為 (B)「你一定會遲到」、(C)「如果你早點來就好了」、(D)「請準時到」，和前半句的意思均接不上。

中文裡所說的「難怪你都不緊張」或「怪不得
會發生這種事情」，英文裡就是用這個句型來表達
恍然大悟的心情。

 關鍵句型 **點**

❶ 這是一個it引導的句型，表示「難怪」、「怪不得」。在口語
中，It is... that可以省略，即：no wonder...，意思也是「難
怪」、「怪不得」。

例 **It is no wonder** you can't sleep. →難怪你睡不著。

No wonder I didn't see her just now.

→難怪我剛才沒看見她。

No wonder you didn't recognize me at once.

→難怪你沒有馬上認出我來。

No wonder I didn't see you.

→難怪我沒看見你。

No wonder you can't come.

→難怪你不能來。

❷ 另外，再告訴大家一個類似的句型，只要將no wonder裡的no換
成small, little，即：(It is) small / little wonder that...，意思和句
型(It is)no wonder that...差不多。

例 **Small wonder** you were late! →怪不得你來得這麼晚！

會話演練 **線**

(It is) no wonder (that)...

A I can't sleep.	A: 我睡不著。
B You had two cups of coffee an hour ago. **It is no wonder** you can't sleep.	B: 你一個小時前喝了兩杯咖啡，難怪你睡不著。

A She didn't accept our invitation to the ball.	A: 她沒有接受我們舞會的邀請。
B **No wonder** I didn't see her.	B: 難怪我沒看見她。

A I left my glasses at home.	A: 我把我的眼鏡忘在家裡了。
B **No wonder** you didn't recognize me at once.	B: 難怪你沒有馬上認出我來。

A I was caught in a traffic jam this morning.	A: 今天早上我遇上了交通堵塞。
B **Small wonder** you were late!	B: 難怪你這麼晚來！

例句**一連發**

❶ It is no wonder you were so late.
難怪你這麼晚才來。

❷ It is no wonder that he didn't want to go.
= **No wonder** he didn't want to go.
難怪他不願去。

❸ No wonder he is not hungry; he has been eating all day.
難怪他不餓，他整天都在吃。

❹ No wonder you couldn't open the door. It was locked.
難怪你打不開這扇門。它鎖住了。

❺ It is no wonder that she has passed the exam.
難怪她考試及格了。

❻ No wonder you speak English so fluently.
難怪你的英文如此流利。

❼ He had made a thorough investigation.
No wonder he knew so much about it.
他進行了徹底的調查，難怪他對此很瞭解。

( ) ❶ –Brad was Jane's brother!
　　–_____ he reminded me so much of Jane!
　　(A) No doubt　　　　(B) Above all
　　(C) No wonder　　　(D) Of course

( ) ❷ Lin is very smart and studies hard as well.It's no _____
　　he always gets the first place in any examination.
　　(A) question　　　　(B) doubt
　　(C) problem　　　　(D) wonder

( ) ❸ –_____.
　　–No wonder no one has arrived yet!
　　(A) The meeting has already started
　　(B) The meeting has been postponed
　　(C) No one is here today
　　(D) Everyone is waiting for you

Answer: **C、D、B**

❶ 句子意思是「布萊德是珍的哥哥。」「難怪他一直讓我想起珍。」
No wonder 是 It is no wonder that 的省略說法，意思是「難怪，
怪不得」。No doubt 是「毫無疑問」，Above all 是「首先」，
Of course 是「當然」，三者都不符合題意，所以答案為 (C)。

❷ 句子意思是：「林很聰明而且很用功。怪不得他每次考試都是
第一名。」It is no wonder that... 表示「難怪，怪不得」的意思。
that 可以省略。所以選 (D)。

❸ 句子的意思是：「會議延期了。」「難怪還沒有人到！」由後
句的意思可判斷最適合的前句為 (B)。其他的選項意為 (A)「會
議已經開始了。」、(C)「今天都沒有人來這裡。」、(D)「大
家都在等你。」，邏輯上無法與答句搭配。

Unit 04 It takes (sb.) ＋ 時間段＋ to ＋ V....

中文裡的「某人花了多少時間做某件事情」就是用這個句型，例如：「我花了三個小時才把這件事情完成」或「你打算花多少時間做這件事情？」。

關鍵句型 點

❶ 這個句型的意思是「做某事花了多長時間」。其中 it 是虛主詞，代替真正主詞，而真正的主詞是後面的不定詞 to ＋ V。take 表示「佔用、花費」時間。而要進一步表示「做某事花費了某人多長的時間」，其句型是：It takes ＋ sb. ＋一段時間＋ to ＋ V。

❷ 這個句型的時態變化表現在 take，可以有 takes（現在簡單式），took（過去簡單式），will take（未來簡單式）三種時態變化：

・It takes (sb.) ＋一段時間＋ to ＋ V

例 **It takes** time **to** translate a difficult article like this.
→翻譯這種難懂的文章需要時間。

・It took (sb.) ＋一段時間＋ to ＋ V

例 **It took me** just ten minutes **to** solve this problem.
→我只花了十分鐘就把這個問題解決了。

・It will take (sb.) ＋一段時間＋ to ＋ V

例 **It will take** at least one year **to** build it.
→至少需要花一年的時間才能建好。

❸ 這個句型中的時間提問要用 how long，即：How long does/did/will it take (sb.) to ＋ V？，意思是：「（某人）做某事花了多長時間？」

例 How long **did it take** you to drive **to** the museum?
→你花了多長時間開車去博物館？

會話翻譯

It takes (sb.) ＋時間段＋ to ＋ V....

A I heard the stadium can't be built in just several months.

B Of course. **It will take** at least one year **to** build it.

A: 聽說這個體育場在幾個月內無法建成。

B: 當然。至少需要花一年的時間才能建好。

A Can you translate the article as quickly as possible?

B **It takes** time **to** translate a difficult article like this.

A: 你可以盡可能快點翻譯完這篇文章嗎？

B: 翻譯這種難懂的文章需要時間。

A **It took me** just ten minutes **to** solve this problem.

B You are so clever.

A: 我只花了十分鐘就把這個問題解決了。

B: 你太聰明了。

A How long **did it take** you **to** drive to the museum?

B About half an hour.

A: 你花了多長時間開車去博物館？

B: 大概半個小時。

例句**一連發**

❶ It takes half an hour to get to the hospital by bus.
坐公車去醫院要花半個小時的時間。

❷ It will take five days to complete the journey.
完成這次旅程將需要五天時間。

❸ It takes me forty minutes to drive to his house.
開車去他家要花我四十分鐘。

❹ It takes me an hour to walk there.
我步行到那裡需要一小時。

❺ It took him three hours to finish his homework.
他花三個小時完成作業。

❻ It will take the workers over a year to build the bridge.
建造這座橋將花費工人們一年多的時間。

❼ It took me two years to finish my studies.
我花了兩年的時間完成學業。

❽ It took us a week to prepare for the party.
我們花了一個星期準備這場派對。

( ) ❶ –It took _____ to draw the picture for you.
　　 –Thank you. It's very kind of you and I like it very
　　　 much.
　　 (A) my two days' time 　　　 (B) two days
　　 (C) two days of my 　　　　 (D) me two days

( ) ❷ _____ did it take you _____ our office?
　　 (A) How long / to find 　　 (B) How often / to find
　　 (C) When / finding 　　　　 (D) How / finding

( ) ❸ _____ a minute to dress myself.
　　 (A) It took me 　　　　　　 (B) It took my
　　 (C) It took you 　　　　　　 (D) It took us

Level

2

It takes (sb.) ＋時間段＋ to ＋ V....

Answer: **D、A、A**

❶ 句子意思是「我花了兩天時間為你畫這幅畫。」「謝謝你。你
真是太好了。我很喜歡這幅畫。」從第二個人的答謝語可以看
出句子中除了要有花費的「時間」外，還需要有「人稱」，即
說明是「我」花費時間畫了這幅畫，所以答案選(D)。

❷ 句子意思是「你花了多少時間才找到我們的辦公室？」句型It
took (sb.) some time to do sth. 的疑問句形式是how long（多
長時間）：How long did it take sb. to do sth.?。而how often是
用來問頻率，即「多久一次」；when是用來問具體的時間點，
即「什麼時候」；how是用來問方式手段，即「如何」，都不
符合。而且take後面要接不定詞，因此(A)為正確答案。

❸ 句子的意思是：「我花了一分鐘穿好衣服。」只要搞清楚句子
的主詞是誰（由後面出現反身動詞 myself 判斷只可能是「我」，
不會是別人），就可以選出正確答案 (A)。

Why not...?

我們常說的「為什麼不把燈打開呢？」或「何不把痛苦的往事給忘了？」，雖然表面上是詢問對方，但其實是給對方建議，在英文裡，Why not...?這個句型也有相同的含意。

關鍵句型 **點**

❶ 這個句型是一個很有用的日常用語，是說話人向對方提出一個建議或勸說，意思是「何不……？」、「為什麼不……？」其實它是一個省略形式的問句。Why not後面要接原形動詞，即「Why not do sth.?」句型中的not代替的是don't you或don't we。可以這樣說，Why not...?句型與Why don't you / Why don't we...?句型為同義句型，也就是說是Why don't you / Why don't we...?句型的簡略形式。

例 **Why not** write a love letter to her?

→為什麼不寫封情書給她？

❷ Why not?也可以單獨使用，用來表示一種驚奇、不滿的反問，可以譯為「為什麼不呢？」。

例 **Why not**? It will be more fun to go this way.

→為什麼不呢？走這條路會更有趣。

會話翻譯

A Why not write a love letter to her?

B I'm not good with words.

A: 為什麼不寫封情書給她？

B: 我的文筆不好。

A Let's go shopping now!

B Sounds wonderful! **Why not?** Let's go.

A: 去購物吧！

B: 太棒了！為什麼不呢？我們走吧。

A Why not have dinner on the lake?

B That sounds like a great idea.

A: 我們為什麼不在湖上用餐呢？

B: 聽起來是個好主意。

A Let's not go this way.

B Why not? It will be more fun to go this way.

A: 我們別走這條路吧。

B: 為什麼不呢？走這條路會更有趣。

A I don't like you.

B Why not?

A: 我不喜歡你。

B: 為什麼？

例句一連發

❶ Why not take a rest in the KFC?
=**Why don't we** take a rest in the KFC?
我們為何不在肯德基休息一下子呢？

❷ Why not match this handbag with your beautiful dress?
=**Why don't you** match this handbag with your beautiful dress?
為何不用這個手提包來搭配你這條漂亮的裙子呢？

❸ Why not have a party on your birthday?
=**Why don't you** have a party on your birthday?
你生日那天何不開一個派對？

❹ Why not see a doctor?
=**Why don't you** see a doctor?
為什麼不去看醫生？

❺ Why not listen to the music quietly?
=**Why don't you** listen to the music quietly?
為什麼不安靜地聽一聽這音樂？

❻ You don't like dolphins? **Why not**? They are so cute!
你不喜歡海豚嗎？為什麼呢？牠們那麼可愛！

( ) **❶** – Why not _____ with us?
   – _____ .
   (A) to have dinner / Help yourself
   (B) to have dinner / Good Idea
   (C) have dinner / Because I'm busy
   (D) have dinner / It sounds great

( ) **❷** – I'm afraid I'm not going to pass the test.
   – _____ You're always working hard!
   (A) Why?   (B) Why not?
   (C) Excuse me.   (D) I'm sorry.

Answer: **D、B**

❶ 句子意思是「何不和我們一起吃晚餐呢？」「聽起來這主意不錯。」句型 Why not...? 的意思是「為什麼不……？」。Why not 後面要接原形動詞，即「Why not do sth.?」。因為問這個句型時，並不是要問對方「理由」，而是要向對方提出一個建議或勸説，所以 because I'm busy. 的回答方式是錯誤且不恰當的。答案應該選 (D)。

❷ 句子意思是「恐怕這次我不會通過這次考試。」「為什麼會不通過呢？你一直都很努力啊！」句型 Why not? 可以譯為「為什麼不／沒有呢？」Excuse me. 意思是「對不起，打擾了。」I'm sorry. 意思是「對不起，很抱歉。」放在這裡都不符合。Why not? 單獨使用時可以表示一種驚奇不滿的反問情緒。從題目的語境可以看出，第二個説話者很驚訝，並不相信第一個説話者「不會通過這次考試。」其中的 not 實際上是代替對方前面已説過的具有否定意義的句子，即：not going to pass the test，以避免與前面的重複，所以選 (B)。

What do you think of/about...?

我們在詢問別人的看法時，常會說：「你覺得這個主意怎麼樣？」或「你覺得怎麼樣？」在英文裡就是用這個句型來表達。

關鍵句型 **點**

❶ What do you think of/about...?這個句型在口語中很常見，意思是「你認為……怎麼樣／如何？」這個句型用來詢問對方對某事或某人的看法和態度。

 What do you think of the show "Super star Avenue"?

→你覺得「超級星光大道」這個節目怎麼樣？

What do you think about soap operas?

→你認為肥皂劇怎麼樣？

❷ 其中的介系詞of或about後面要接名詞、代名詞或動名詞。

 What do you think about our logo?

→你覺得我們的標誌怎麼樣？

What do you think of swimming? →你覺得游泳怎麼樣？

會話演練 **線**

會話翻譯

A **What do you think about** soap operas?

B I can't stand them at all.

A: 你認為肥皂劇怎麼樣？

B: 我完全無法忍受它們。

A **What do you think of** Super star Avenue Contestants?

B I like them very much, especially Yoga Lin.

A: 你覺得星光幫怎麼樣？

B: 我很喜歡他們，尤其是林宥嘉。

A **What do you think about** our logo?

B It's very striking.

A: 你覺得我們的標誌怎麼樣？

B: 很醒目。

A **What do you think of** swimming?

B It's a good way to keep fit!

A: 你覺得游泳怎麼樣？

B: 那是個保持健康的好方法。

A **What do you think about** the new restaurant?

B The food is great, the service not so much.

A: 你覺得那家新餐廳怎麼樣？

B: 食物很棒，服務就不怎麼樣。

例句 一連發

❶ What do you think of the movie?
你認為這部電影怎麼樣？

❷ What do you think of my work?
你覺得我的工作做得如何？

❸ What do you think of things like these?
你對這種事有什麼看法？

❹ What do you think of meeting him at the airport?
你覺得到機場去跟他碰面怎麼樣？

❺ What do you think about the concert?
你認為這場演唱會怎麼樣？

❻ What do you think about the ideas they put forward?
你覺得他們提出的意見怎麼樣？

❼ What do you think of this song?
你覺得這首歌怎麼樣？

❽ What do you think about this suggestion?
你覺得這個建議怎麼樣？

小小**試身手**

( ) **❶** –What _____ you _____ her new boyfriend?
　　–I think he is easy-going and handsome.
　　(A) are / thinking　　　(B) are / thinking about
　　(C) do / think　　　　　(D) do / think about

( ) **❷** What do you _____ my suggestion?
　　(A) think　　　　　　　(B) think over
　　(C) think of　　　　　　(D) think out

( ) **❸** What do you think of _____ on a cruise this
　　summer?
　　(A) go　　　　　　　　(B) will go
　　(C) to go　　　　　　　(D) going

Answer: **D、C、D**

❶ 句子意思是「你覺得她新交的男朋友怎麼樣？」「我覺得他很隨和而且長得很帥」。What do you think about ...? 這個句型的意思是「你認為……怎麼樣／如何？」，用來詢問對方對某事或某人的看法和態度等。答案為 (D)。

❷ 句子意思是「你認為我的建議怎麼樣？」think over 是「好好考慮」的意思，think out 是「想出、研究出」的意思，放在題目句子中都不通順，而 What do you think of... 是用來詢問對方對某件事情的看法，所以答案為 (C)。

❸ 句子的意思是：「你覺得今年夏天去搭遊輪怎麼樣？」What do you think of...? 句型中，接下來需要接 V+ing，因此 (D) 為正確答案。

Unit 07 Will/Would you (please)...?

當我們很客氣地請對方做某件事時,我們會說:「請你把音量關小聲一點好嗎?」或「你可以幫我搬這些東西嗎?」,在英文裡就是用這個句型。

 關鍵句型 **點**

❶ 這個句型用於向某人提出詢問、請求,在口語中尤為常見和實用。可以靈活翻譯成「你可以……嗎?」、「可不可以請你……?」等。句中的動詞要用原形動詞。句首的will或would並不代表時態,而只是為了表示禮貌的語氣。需要注意的是would與will的唯一區別就是,would的請求語氣比will更加委婉和客氣,常用於向陌生人提出請求。

❷ 回答這個句型時,如果願意,可以說Yes, I'll be glad to. / Certainly. / Of course.等;如果不願意或不能夠,可以說No, I'm sorry. / Sorry, but...等。

例 –**Would you** stay with me for another day?
→你可以再陪我一天嗎?
–Yes, certainly. →好啊,沒問題!

❸ 如果要加上please,可以將please放在will you的後面或者放在句子末尾。

例 **Would you please** ask him to call me back?
→你可以請他回電話給我嗎?
Will you hold this bag for a moment, **please**?
→你可以幫我拿一下這個包包嗎?

會話演練 線

A Sorry, Mr. White is in a meeting.

B **Would you please** ask him to call me back?

A: 對不起,懷特先生正在開會。

B: 你可以請他回電話給我嗎?

A **Will you** hold this bag for a moment, **please?**

B With pleasure.

A: 你可以拿一下這個包包嗎?

B: 非常樂意。

A **Would you** stay with me for another day?

B Yes, certainly.

A: 你可以再陪我一天嗎?

B: 好啊,沒問題!

A **Would you please** drop me off at the train station?

B Sure, I don't mind.

A: 可以請你載我到火車站嗎?

B: 沒問題,我不介意。

A **Would you please** come with me?

B Depends on where you're going.

A: 可以請你跟我來嗎?

B: 那要看你要去哪裡。

例句 **一連發**

❶ Would you please take me to the hospital?
你可以帶我去醫院嗎？

❷ Would you please look after my dog for two days?
請你照顧我的小狗兩天，可以嗎？

❸ Would you go to school on time, **please?**
請你準時上學，可以嗎？

❹ Will you accept the centract?
你接受這份合約嗎？

❺ Would you please pass me a piece of paper?
你可以遞給我一張紙嗎？

❻ Would you finish the food quickly?
你可以快點把東西吃完嗎？

❼ Will you please shut up for two minutes?
可以請你閉嘴兩分鐘嗎？

❽ Would you take these boxes inside?
你可以把這些箱子拿進去嗎？

小小試身手

( ) ❶ This box is too heavy, _____ give me a hand?
(A) would you mind　(B) would you please
(C) will you like to　(D) will you please to

( ) ❷ Would you_____ the salt, please?
(A) pass me　　　(B) passed me
(C) to pass me　　(D) pass to me

( ) ❸ Will you _____ me?
(A) married　　　(B) to marry
(C) marry　　　　(D) marry to

Will/Would you (please)...?

Answer: **B、A、C**

❶ 句子意思是「這個箱子太重了，你可以幫我嗎？」首先根據句子意思可判斷，說話人是在向別人尋求幫助，would you mind 是「你介意……？」的意思，而且後面要接動名詞。will you like to 不是正確結構；will you please to 也不是正確結構，would you please 是「請你……可以嗎？」因此答案為 (B)。

❷ 句子意思是「請你把鹽遞給我，好嗎？」在 Would you please...? 這個句型中，句首的 would 不表示過去時態，只是為了表示更委婉客氣的請求，後面的動詞要用原形。the salt 和 me 是動詞 pass 的兩個受詞，pass me the salt 或者 pass the salt to me 這兩種說法都可以，因此答案選 (A)。

❸ 句子的意思是：「你願意跟我結婚嗎？」選擇原形動詞 (C) 即可。marry 後面不需要加一個 to，除非前面有 be，形成 be married to（與某人為婚姻關係）。

Unit 08

as ...as possible

中文裡的「儘量」、「儘可能」，就是用這個句型來表達，例如：「請你儘快回信給我」或「我會儘可能幫你完成這件事情」。

 關鍵句型 **點**

這個句型是指達到某種程度或符合某種要求，意思是「盡可能……」，「愈 ...... 愈好」，這個句型還可以說成 as...as one can。可根據需要，在兩個 as 之間使用不同的形容詞或副詞，如下所示：

· as soon as possible	儘快
· as quick as possible	儘快
· as often as possible	儘量經常
· as big as possible	儘可能大
· as carefully as possible	儘可能仔細
· as loudly as possible	儘可能大聲
· as friendly as possible	儘量友善

例 Reply to me **as soon as possible**, please.
→請儘快回覆我。
Please have **as much as possible**. →請儘量多吃一點。
Please read the text **as loudly as possible**.
→請儘可能大聲朗讀這篇文章。

會話演練 線

A Can I think it over?

B Sure. Reply to me **as soon as possible** please.

A: 我可以考慮一下嗎?

B: 可以,請儘快答覆我。

A These dishes you made look yummy.

B If you like them, please have **as much as possible**.

A: 你做的這些菜看起來很美味!

B: 如果你喜歡,就儘量多吃點。

A Please read the text **as loudly as possible**.

B Sorry. I have a sore throat.

A: 請盡可能大聲朗讀這篇文章。

B: 對不起,我喉嚨痛。

A How much wine should I bring?

B **As much as possible**, please.

A: 我應該帶多少酒?

B: 越多越好,拜託。

例句一連發

❶ Go to the doctor **as soon as possible!**
儘快到醫生那裡去！

❷ Bring me **as much as possible.**
儘量帶多一點給我。

❸ I'll return your book **as soon as possible.**
=I'll return your book **as soon as I can.**
我將儘快把你的書還給你。

❹ It's dark. You'd better go back **as early as possible.**
天黑了，你最好儘早回去。

❺ Try to be **as friendly** to others **as possible.**
對別人要儘可能友好。

❻ Your should go home to see your parents **as often as possible.**
=You should go home to see your parents **as often as you can.**
你應該儘可能常回去看你父母。

❼ Get up **as early as possible** tomorrow.
明天請儘早起床。

❽ Will you please say it **as clearly as possible?**
= Will you please say it **as clearly as you can?**
你能儘可能說得清楚些嗎？

小小試身手

( ) ❶ You should try to express your own ideas ＿＿＿.
(A) as clearly as possible
(B) as clear as possible
(C) so clearly as possible
(D) as clear as possibly

( ) ❷ Exercise as ＿＿＿ , and you will stay energetic.
(A) early as possible
(B) possible as early
(C) often as possible
(D) possible as often

( ) ❸ We will get in touch as ＿＿＿＿ as possible.
(A) soonly　　　　　(B) soon
(C) fastly　　　　　(D) latter

Answer: **A**、**C**、**B**

❶ 句子意思是「你應該儘量清楚地表達自己的想法。」as...as possible 是固定結構的句型，在 as...as 之間既可以放形容詞也可以放副詞，但是題目中要修飾的是動詞 express，所以要用副詞 clearly「清楚地」，答案為 (A)。

❷ 句子意思是「儘量經常鍛練身體，這樣你就會精力充沛。」as...as possible 表示「儘可能……」的意思。而要表示做某事的頻率「經常」，要用副詞 often，所以選 (C)。

❸ 句子的意思是：「我們會盡快跟你聯絡。」空格內需填入用來修飾 get in touch（動詞片語）的字，因此應為副詞，而選項中唯一正確的副詞就是 (B)，正確答案。(A) 和 (C) 並無此字，而 latter 指的是「之後的」，和句意無關。

...as soon as...

當我們說「一……就……」例如──「我一看到她，就呆掉了」或「老師一進來，全班就安靜了」，強調一件事情緊接著一件事情發生時，就可以用這個句型。

 關鍵句型 **點**

❶ as soon as... 表示「一……就……」。as soon as... 後面接的句子通常用現在式表示未來的時間，換言之，不能用未來式，但是 as soon as... 前面的主句可用現在式、過去式或未來式。

例 I'll inform you **as soon as** I know the result.
→我一知道結果就告訴你。

❷ as soon as... 可與句型 the moment (that)/ the minute (that) / immediately 互換，也表示「一……就……」。

例 I knew that there was no hope **the moment** I heard what he said. →我一聽到他說的話，我就知道沒希望了。

❸ on sth./on doing sth. 也表示「一……就……」、「當……」。

例 **On** hearing the news of her mother's death, she burst into tears. →她一聽到她母親的死訊，就大哭起來。

會話演練 線

A Please tell me the result as soon as possible.

B Ok! I'll inform you **as soon as** I know the result.

A: 請儘快告訴我結果。

B: 好的，我一知道結果就告訴你。

A When did you fall in love with her?

B I fell in love with her **the minute** I saw her.

A: 你什麼時候愛上她的？

B: 我一見到她就愛上她了。

A I knew that there was no hope **the moment** I heard what he said.

B But you should have tried again.

A: 我一聽見他說的話我就知道沒希望了。

B: 但是你應該再試一下的。

A **On** hearing the news of her mother's death, she burst into tears.

B What can we do for her?

A: 她一聽到她母親的死訊，就大哭起來。

B: 我們能為她做點什麼嗎？

例句一連發

1 I recognized her **as soon as** I saw her.
我一看見她就立刻認出她來。

2 As soon as the lessons were over, the children hurried to the playground.
一下課，孩子們就奔向遊樂場。

3 Call me **as soon as** you get off the bus.
你一下公車就打電話給我。

4 We'll tell the manager the news **as soon as** he comes back to the office.
經理一回辦公室，我們就會告訴他這個消息。

5 He felt a thrill **the moment that** he got into the theater.
他一進入劇院就感到一陣激動。

6 She married a rich man **the minute** she graduated from college.
她一從大學畢業就嫁給一個有錢人。

7 As soon as you leave this tent, you will get a big surprise.
你一走出帳篷，便會大吃一驚。

8 The moment I saw him I knew he was your ex–boyfriend.
我一看到他就知道他是你的前男友。

9 On arriving at the village, we were warmly welcomed by the villagers.
我們一到那個村莊，就受到村民們的熱烈歡迎。

小小 試身手

(　)❶ I'll call you ____ I ____ news on him.
(A) as soon as / will get
(B) the minute / will get
(C) as soon as / get
(D) the moment / will get

(　)❷ –Did you remember to give Mary the money you owed her?
–Yes, I gave it to her ____ I saw her.
(A) while　　　　　(B) the moment
(C) suddenly　　　(D) once

(　)❸ _____ saw her, I fell in love.
(A) On　　　　　　(B) The moment
(C) On I　　　　　(D) The moment I

Answer: C、B、D

❶ 句子意思是「我一得到他的消息就打電話給你。」這裡要注意的是，as soon as... 和 the minute (that)...、the moment (that)...，它們都可以表示「一……就……」。主句可以是一般未來式，但是子句通常要用現在簡單式代替未來簡單式，故只能選 (C)。

❷ 句子意思是「你記得把欠瑪麗的錢還給她嗎？」「是的，我記得。我一見到她就把錢還她了。」四個選項中，只有 the moment 可作連接詞，意為「一……就……」。 故最佳選項為 (B)。

❸ 句子的意思是：「我一看到她，就愛上她了。」此處需選 (D) 才是正確的句型，若要用 On 作為句子的開頭，則要把後面改成 On seeing her... 才正確。

Unit 10

so ＋助動詞＋主詞

要附和別人的說法時，我們會說：「我也是」或「我也不是」，這時候，就可以用這個句型來表達。

關鍵句型 點

❶ 句型「so ＋助動詞＋主詞」用來表示「……也一樣」、「……也是如此」。這個句型中的主詞並非指上句主詞所代表的人或物，而是指另外一個人或物。其中的助動詞就用來代替上句的全部動作內容，所以要與其後面的主詞保持時態和單複數的一致。so 後面是典型的部分倒裝。

 Well, I had a really good time. →嗯，我玩得很開心。
So did I. →我也一樣。

❷ 句型「neither/nor ＋助動詞＋主詞」與上面句型相對應，用來表示某人（物）具有與前者相同的否定情況，意為「……也不……」。

 I haven't been to Beijing. →我沒去過北京。
Neither have I. →我也沒去過。

❸ 有一個與「so ＋助動詞＋主詞」容易混淆的句型：「so ＋主詞＋助動詞」。這個句型是個強調句型，用來表示贊同對方的話語，意為「……確實如此」。其中的主詞與上句所提到的是同一個人或物。so 後面是直述，而不是倒裝。

 Your brother studies very hard. →你弟弟很用功。
So he does. →他的確是這樣。

會話演練 **線**

A Well, I had a really good time.

B **So did I.**

A: 嗯，我玩得很開心。

B: 我也一樣。

A I'm sorry you can't go for an outing with us, John.

B **So am I,** John.

A: 約翰，很遺憾你不能跟我們一起去郊遊。

B: 我也很遺憾，約翰。

A I haven't been to Beijing.

B **Neither have I.**

A: 我沒去過北京。

B: 我也沒去過。

A Your brother studies very hard.

B **So he does.**

A: 你弟弟很用功。

B: 他的確是這樣。

A I have never won the lottery before.

B Neither have I.

A: 我從來沒中過樂透。

B: 我也沒有。

例句 一連發

1 She cried, and **so did the others**.
她哭了，其他人也哭了。

2 He was a smoker. **So was his wife**.
他以前會抽煙，他妻子也一樣。

3 They are now preparing for their final examinations; **so are we**.
他們正在為期末考試作準備，我們也一樣。

4 If they can finish the job, **so can I**.
如果他們能完成這項工作，我也能。

5 The society has changed and **so have the people in it**.
社會變了，社會裡的人也變了。

6 She seldom goes to the cinema; **neither does he.**
她很少去看電影，他也一樣。

7 You don't want to take the responsibility; **neither do I.**
你不想擔這個責任，我也不想。

8 The first one wasn't good and **nor was the second one.**
第一個不好，第二個也不好。

9 I can't swim, and **nor can she.**
我不會游泳，她也不會。

小小試身手

( ) **❶** Mike knows a lot about the Internet. And _____.
(A) I don't, either　　(B) so do I
(C) so am I　　(D) I am, too

( ) **❷** –I don't think I can walk any further.
　–_____. Let's stop here for a rest.
(A) Neither am I　　(B) Neither can I
(C) I don't think so　　(D) I think so

( ) **❸** –Your dog sure sleeps a lot.
　–_____.
(A) So does I　　(B) I am, too
(C) So he does　　(D) He does, either

Answer: **B、B、C**

❶ 句子意思是「麥克懂很多關於網路的東西，我也一樣。」「so ＋助動詞＋主詞」表示前面句子所說的情況也適用於後一句的主詞。這裡要用助動詞do代替前面一句所指的內容，也就是代表I know a lot about the Internet, too.，所以答案選(B)。

❷ 句子意思是「我覺得我再也無法往前走了。」「我也走不動了。我們在這裡休息一下吧。」第一個人用否定的句型表達了I can't walk any further的含義。第二個人和他有同樣的感覺，意思是I can't walk any further, either.，所以才建議停下來稍作休息。Neither...表示某人（物）具有與前者相同的否定情況，意為「……也不……」，故答案為(B)。

❸ 句子的意思是：「你的狗真能睡啊。」「牠確實很能睡。」，(C) 為正確答案。此處或許也可以用 (A) 中的 So do... 或 So does... 的句型表示「（某人）也很能睡」，但 does 和 I 動詞與主詞無法搭配，因此不可選。

107

Unit 11 It be ＋時間段＋ before...

當我們說「我花了二小時才到達目的地」或「還要再過三個月她才會過來看我們」，表示要花多少時間才會達成某件事，就是用這個句型。

 關鍵句型 **點**

❶ 句型「It be＋時間段＋before＋子句」中表示時間段的詞語通常有a long time, (one, two, three...) years/months/days/minutes 等。before引導的子句中通常用現在簡單式表示未來的時間。

例 It was only four days **before** she finished the work.
　→她只用了四天就完成了那份工作。

❷ 當主句中的動詞是肯定時，可以翻譯成「過了……（時間）才能……」、「在……（時間）之後才……」。

例 It will be six months **before** we meet again.
　→六個月後我們才能再見面。

❸ 當主句中的動詞是否定時，可以翻譯成「不到……（時間）就……」。

例 It was not half an hour **before** I completed my English writing. →不到半個小時我就寫完了我的英文作文。

會話演練 **線**

A **It was** only four days **before** she finished the work.	A: 她只用了四天就完成了那個工作。
B Well, that was very fast.	B: 喔，還真快啊。

A **It was** a long time **before** the police arrived.	A: 警察好久以後才趕到。
B You should have called 110 earlier.	B: 你應該早一點打 110 的。

A **It will be** six months **before** we meet again.	A: 六個月後我們才能再見。
B I will write to you often.	B: 我會經常給你寫信的。

A **It was not** half an hour **before** I completed my English writing.	A: 不到半個小時我就寫完了我的英文作文。
B No wonder you made so many mistakes.	B: 難怪你犯了這麼多的錯誤。

It be ＋時間段＋ before...

例句 **一連發**

❶ It is only several minutes **before** the boy works out the difficult problem.
那個小男孩只用了幾分鐘就把這道題解出來了。

❷ It was years **before** he returned.
過了好多年他才回來。

❸ It was four hours **before** the fire was put out.
四個小時之後大火才被撲滅。

❹ It was a long time **before** I fell asleep.
過了很久，我才睡著。

❺ It will be five years before we meet again.
五年以後我們才能再見。

❻ It was an hour **before** he finished his homework.
一個小時以後他才做完家庭作業。

❼ It was long **before** he gave me an answer.
過了好久他才答覆我。

❽ It will not be a week **before** I visit you.
不到一星期，我就會去拜訪你了。

( ) ❶ It was some time ____ we realized the truth.
   (A) when　　　　(B) until
   (C) since　　　　(D) before

( ) ❷ It will be several months ____ they get used to the work.
   (A) when　　　　(B) after
   (C) that　　　　(D) before

( ) ❸ It _____ some time before he wakes up. You'll have to wait.
   (A) had been　　(B) was
   (C) is　　　　　(D) will be

Answer: **D**、**D**、**D**

❶ 句子的意思是「過了一段時間後，我們才瞭解到事情的真相。」some time 表示「一段時間」，根據題意和時態，可判斷只有 before 符合題意，可以翻譯成「過一段時間後才……」。正確答案是 (D)。

❷ 句子的意思是「還要好幾個月的時間他們才能習慣這份工作。」several months 是時間段，表示子句動作所花費的時間。四個選項中只有 before 可以表示「要過……（時間）才……」，所以選 (D)。

❸ 句子的意思是：「還要過一陣子他才會起來，你得等等了。」由後句用了未來式判斷，句中的「他」應該還沒醒來，他醒來應該是未來的事，因此選擇 (D) 為正確答案。

It be ＋ not long before...

我們常說的「不久之後」，可以用這個句型來
表達，例如：「不久之後，我就把這件事情忘了」
或「要不了多久，敵軍就會投降的」。

 關鍵句型 **點**

❶ 句型「It be ＋ not long before ＋子句」，意思是「不久就……」。
當強調主句所表達的時間不長、花費力氣小的時候，該句型
的含義與 before long 相近，都可以表示「不久……」、「很
快……」。

例 **It won't be long before** I know the result of the experiment.
→要不了多久我就可以知道實驗的結果。

It was not long before the ambulance arrived
→沒過多久救護車就來了。

It will not be long before the truth comes out.
→不久後真相就會大白了。

會話演練 線

A How are you getting on with the experiment?

B **It won't be long before** I know the result of the experiment.

A: 你的實驗進行的怎麼樣了？

B: 不用多久我就可以知道實驗結果了。

A **It was not long before** the ambulance arrived.

B Lucky.

A: 沒過多久救護車就來了。

B: 真幸運！

A I can't tell whether the news is true.

B **It will not be long before** the truth comes out.

A: 我不知道這個消息是真是假。

B: 不久真相就會大白。

A How long do we have to wait?

B **It won't be long before** he arrives. Just wait and see.

A: 我們得等多久？

B: 他不久後就會到了，你等著看。

例句**一連發**

❶ It was not long before the movie star appeared.
不久這個電影明星就出現了。

❷ It won't be long before you get well.
要不了多久，你就會好的。

❸ It won't be long before we finish the work.
我們很快就會完成這項工作。

❹ It was not long before he sensed the danger he was in.
不久他就意識到他處境的危險。

❺ It won't be long before they understand each other.
他們不久就會互相瞭解的。

❻ It won't be long before you reach your goal.
你離達成目標不遠了。

❼ It was not long before a helicopter arrived on the scene to rescue the survivors of the plane crash.
直升機不久就到現場去援救飛機墜毀後的生還者。

❽ It will not be long before you regret what you have done.
不用多久你就會對你的所作所為感到後悔。

❾ It won't be long before we work out some plans to improve our work.
要不了多久我們就會制定好一些計畫來改善我們的工作。

小小試身手

(　)❶ It was not long _____ I forgot it all.
(A) then　　　　　(B) when
(C) after　　　　　(D) before

(　)❷ Don't worry! It _____ be long _____ you get used to wearing glasses.
(A) wasn't / before　(B) won't / before
(C) wasn't / after　　(D) won't / that

(　)❸ It _____ long before he got hungry and went out for a snack.
(A) can't be　　　　(B) wasn't
(C) won't be　　　　(D) isn't

Answer: D、B、B

❶ 句子的意思是「沒過多久我就把這一切都忘了。」句型「It be + not long before +子句」，意思是「不久……就……。」所以正確答案選 (D)。

❷ 句子的意思是「別擔心！不久後你就會習慣戴眼鏡的。」根據題意，首先排除 (C)、(D)。再根據 Don't worry 可知習慣戴眼鏡應該是以後的事，所以主句的動詞用未來式，正確答案是 (B)。

❸ 句子的意思是：「過不了多久他就餓了，出去外面找點心吃。」由後面的 got 與 went 等動詞，可判斷句子為過去式，選擇唯一的過去式 (B) 為正確答案。

Unit 13 及物動詞＋人／物 ＋形容詞

在英文裡，有一些及物動詞可以用在這個句型當中，例如 make, believe, consider 等，就如同中文裡所說的「把它弄乾淨」或「相信這是真的」或「認為他很帥」等。

 關鍵句型點

❶ 句型「及物動詞＋人/物＋形容詞」中的受詞可以是人或物，也可以用名詞或代名詞充當，但其後面要接形容詞當作補語，用來說明受詞的狀態或變化的結果。

❷ 常用於本句型的及物動詞有：believe, consider, think, color, cut, dye, drive, find, get, lay, strike, have, hold, wash, imagine, judge, keep, leave, make, paint, turn, set, prove, wish等。

例 They **painted the wall red**. →他們把牆漆成了紅色。

Keep the kids quiet, please. →請讓孩子們安靜下來。

I **wish you well and happy**. →祝你健康快樂。

會話演練 **線**

A What **makes you so angry?**

B They **painted the wall red**.

A: 是什麼讓你這麼生氣？

B: 他們把牆漆成了紅色。

A **Keep the kids quiet,** please.

B They are too excited to control themselves.

A: 請讓孩子們安靜下來。

B: 他們太興奮了，無法控制自己。

A I **wish you well and happy.**

B The same to you.

A: 祝你健康快樂。

B: 你也是。

A You should **dye your hair pink**.

B That's not a bad idea.

A: 你應該把頭髮染成粉紅色。

B: 好像是個好主意。

A Please **leave me alone**.

B OKay, we can talk later.

A: 請讓我自己一個人靜一靜。

B: 好，我們待會再聊。

及物動詞＋人／物＋形容詞

117

例句一連發

❶ We must **keep our classroom clean.**
我們必須讓教室保持乾淨。

❷ The girl **dyed her hair purple.**
這個女孩把頭髮染成了紫色。

❸ We all **imagine him foolish.**
我們都以為他很傻。

❹ The storm **kept everyone indoors.**
暴風雨把所有人都困在屋子裡。

❺ Do you **consider the man honest?**
你覺得這個人誠實嗎？

❻ You're almost **driving me crazy.**
你幾乎要把我逼瘋了。

❼ I will **prove it true.**
我會證明這是真的。

❽ **Color the apple red** and **color the banana yellow.**
把蘋果塗成紅色，把香蕉塗成黃色。

小小試身手

( ) ❶ She found the movie _____.
(A) interest　　　　(B) interests
(C) interesting　　　(D) interestingly

( ) ❷ –What do you think of Mr. Smith?
–I _____ him _____.
(A) considered / capable
(B) consider / very capable
(C) considered / able
(D) consider / capably

( ) ❸ I was surprised that your friend did such a stupid thing.
I had _____ him quite smart.
(A) proven　　　　(B) imagined
(C) gotten　　　　(D) wished

Answer: C、B、B

❶ 這個句子的意思是「她發覺這部電影很有趣。」句型「及物動詞＋人／物＋形容詞」中，find 後面要接形容詞當作受詞 the movie 的補語。interest 是名詞，interestingly 是副詞，所以排除。只有 interesting 是形容詞，所以正確答案是 (C)。

❷ 這個句子的意思是「你認為史密斯先生怎麼樣？」「我認為他很有能力。」從對話情境來看，詢問對方看法，對方回答的也是現在的看法，所以要用現在簡單式。consider 後面要接形容詞 capable 作受詞 him 的補語，表示「他」是「有能力的」，所以正確答案是 (B)。

❸ 句子的意思是：「我很驚訝你朋友做了這種蠢事。我還以為他很聰明。」對方聰不聰明，是很難由「我」來「證明」或「達成」的，因此 (A) 和 (C) 都不對，而一般不會沒事去誠摯地「希望」別人的朋友（還不是自己的朋友）很聰明，所以(D)也不對。在此為「想、認為」的 (B) 為正確答案。

Level 2 過關大挑戰

1 He hasn't slept at all for three days. _____ he is tired out.
   (A) There is no point
   (B) There is no need
   (C) It is no wonder
   (D) It is no way

2 What's _____ matter _____ your computer?
   (A) the / with
   (B) a / with
   (C) the / in
   (D) a / in

3 What do you think about _____ in public?
   (A) to smoke
   (B) smoke
   (C) smoking
   (D) I smoke

4 I'll go home as soon as the meeting _____.
   (A) will end
   (B) ends
   (C) ending
   (D) ended

5 It will take three hours _____ the report.
   (A) on
   (B) that I can write
   (C) in writing
   (D) to write

6 Why not _____ my advice?
   (A) listened to
   (B) to listen to
   (C) listen to
   (D) listening to

❼ Jenny was very angry at what you said, and _____.

(A) so was I   (B) so did I

(C) so I was   (D) so I did

❽ Lily hasn't been to Japan, and ____.

(A) so is her husband

(B) so has her husband

(C) neither have her husband

(D) nor has her husband

❾ Mary promised to help me and ____ the next day.

(A) so did she   (B) so she did

(C) so will she   (D) so she will

❿ I hope that I can meet you again ____.

(A) so soon as possibly   (B) as soon as possibly

(C) so soon as possible   (D) as soon as possible

⓫ – I'm sorry I'm late again.

– ____. But come to school earlier next time.

(A) You are welcome   (B) Don't worry

(C) It doesn't matter   (D) No problem

超詳細解析

❶ 句子意思是「他連續三天沒睡覺。難怪他會累垮。」It is no wonder (that)...句型表示「難怪，怪不得」的意思。There is no point是「沒有意義」；There is no need是「沒有必要。」；It is no way是「辦不到。」很顯然，答案選(C)。

❷ 句型What's the matter with... ?」表示「……怎麼了？」、「……出什麼毛病了？」它是表達對對方的關心或詢問一些事物或狀況，句型中的 what 是主詞，matter是「問題」、「毛病」。the matter在意義和用法上相當於形容詞wrong。後面的介系詞要用with。所以正確答案是(A)。

❸ 句型What do you think about ...? 用來詢問對方對某事或某人的看法和態度等，意思是「你認為……怎麼樣／如何？」介系詞about後面要接名詞、代名詞或動名詞。所以要用smoke（抽煙）的動名詞形式smoking，答案選(C)。

❹ 句型as soon as...意為「一……就……」。在這個句型中，主句可以是一般未來式，但是子句通常要用現在簡單式代替未來簡單式，故只能選(B)。

❺ It takes/took/will take (sb.)＋一段時間＋to do sth.這個句型表示「做某事花了（某人）多長時間。」其中it是虛主詞，而真主詞是後面的不定詞to do sth.，所以正確答案選(D)。

❻ Why not後面要接原形動詞，即「Why not do sth.?」，意思是 「為什麼不……？」是說話人向對方提出建議或勸說。選項中只有listen to是原形動詞，所以選(C)。

❼ 句型「so＋be動詞＋主詞」表示前面句子所說的情況也適用於後一句的主詞。這裡要用be動詞was代替前一句所指的內容，即：I was angry at what you said, too.而「so＋主詞＋助動詞/be動詞」句型結構，用於對上面的說

話內容表示贊同，意為「……確實如此」。在這裡顯然不是這個意思，而是「珍妮對你說的話很生氣，我也一樣。」所以正確答案是(A)。

⑧ 本題的句子意思是「莉莉沒有去過日本，她老公也沒有去過。」前半句是否定，後半句要表達的是：Her husband hasn't been to Japan, either.。neither/nor...表示某人（物）具有與前者相同的否定情況，意為「……也不……」。其次，因為her husband是第三人稱，助動詞要用has，所以選(D)。

⑨ 從結構上來看，前一句的主詞Mary和後一句的主詞she是同一個人；從句子的意思來看，要表達的是「瑪麗答應要幫我，第二天她確實就這樣做了（幫我了）。」所以要用「so＋主詞＋助動詞」，用於對上面的說話內容表示贊同，意為「……確實如此」。正確答案是(B)。

⑩ 句子意思是「我希望我可以盡快與你再次碰面。」as...as possible句型表示「儘可能……」。所以選(D)。

⑪ 從對話判斷，第二個說話者接受了第一個說話者的道歉，同時藉由but引出句子，表達希望第一個說話者「下次早點到學校」。You are welcome是「不客氣」；Don't worry是「別擔心」；No problem是「沒問題」；It doesn't matter是「沒關係」，最符合上下文意思。所以最佳答案是(C)。

過關測驗解答

01~06: (C)(A)(C)(B)(D)(C)   07~11: (A)(D)(B)(D)(C)

Level 2
補充文法面

直述句 2 大結構，疑問句 4 大類型

在英文中，依照使用目的，可以將句子分為直述句、疑問句、祈使句和感嘆句四類。要想瞭解英文的基本句型，就要先瞭解句子的分類。現在，我們就先來瞭解直述句與疑問句。

1▶直述句

直述句的作用，是用來說明一個事實或是陳述說話人的看法；又可分成肯定直述句和否定直述句。

1.肯定直述句有以下兩種結構：

★ 主詞＋動詞＋（受詞）

需要注意的是，如果動詞是及物動詞，後面則需要接受詞；如果是不及物動詞，後面則不能接受詞，而如果想要接受詞，就需要加入介系詞。

例如：I like cartoons. 我喜歡卡通片。（主詞＋及物動詞＋受詞）
　　　She smiles. 她露出微笑。（主詞＋不及物動詞）
　　　They live in Taipei. 他們住在台北。
　　　（主詞＋不及物動詞＋介系詞＋受詞）

★ 主詞＋連綴動詞＋補語

這個結構表示的是主詞的特徵、屬性、身份、狀態等。常見的連綴動詞有：be, get, become, grow, come, go, seem, remain, keep, look, feel, taste, sound, smell等。

例如：My father is a lawyer. 我的父親是一位律師。

He became a famous director later.

他後來成為一位著名的導演。

其中尤其需要注意的是，感官動詞look, feel, taste, sound, smell 用作連綴動詞時，後面可接形容詞或名詞作補語，且這個句型中的補語不能是副詞。很多人經常犯這種錯誤，所以一定要注意哦！

例：Your face **feels** cold. 你的臉摸起來很冷。

The apple **tastes** sour. 這個蘋果嚐起來真酸。

You **look** good. 你看起來不錯。

It **sounds** a good idea. 這聽起來是個好主意。

2.否定直述句有以下四種結構：

★ 主詞＋**do/does/did**＋**not**＋原形動詞（一般動詞的否定句）

例：I **don't** like hamburger. 我不喜歡漢堡。

★ 主詞＋**be動詞**＋**not**＋…（be動詞的否定句）

例：She **wasn't** at home during that time. 她那段時間不在家。

★ 主詞＋**will/have/has...**＋**not**＋…（助動詞的否定句）

例：He **hasn't** come back yet. 他還沒回來。

The old machine **will not** be repaired any more.

這台老機器再也不會被修理了。

★主詞＋**can/may/must/could/would...**＋**not**＋原形動詞（情態動詞的否定句）

例：My mother **can't** surf the Internet. 我媽媽不會上網。

You **mustn't** miss the movie. 你一定不能錯過這部電影。

最後，要強調的是，直述句的結構是先主詞、再動詞，如果有受詞的話，後接受詞。這種結構中呈現的語序就是英文中的基本語序，也就是自然語序。掌握直述句的結構和語序，是接下來學習疑問句、倒裝句等結構和語序的基礎。

2 疑問句

疑問句是用來提出問題的句子。和中文一樣，英文的疑問句句尾要用問號。英文的疑問句分為一般疑問句、特殊疑問句、選擇疑問句和反意疑問句四種。

1.一般疑問句

★ **be動詞＋主詞＋…?**

例：Are you hungry? 你餓了嗎？

★ **助動詞＋主詞＋…?**

例：Did he pass the test yesterday? 他通過昨天的測驗了嗎？

Have you been to Taipei recently? 你最近去過台北嗎？

★ **情態動詞＋主詞＋原形動詞＋…?**

例：Can I help you? 我能幫你嗎？

Need you go there so soon? 你需要這麼早就去那裡嗎？

★ **助動詞或情態動詞的否定縮寫＋主詞＋…?**

可以看出，一般疑問句的語序與直述句的語序不同，在英文中，這稱為倒裝語序。

最後一種形式又被稱為否定疑問句。它通常以助動詞或情態動詞的否定形式開頭，常見的有can't, won't, aren't等……，主詞多是第二人稱。這就構成了英文中常見的否定疑問句句型，常用來表達驚訝、厭煩、懷疑等強烈感情色彩，或向對方提出建議、看法等。

例：Can't you drive a car? 你難道不會開車嗎？

Won't she come? 她不來了嗎？

2.特殊疑問句

特殊疑問句就是針對句子某一部分提問的疑問句，通常以特殊疑問詞開頭，如：who, what, which, where, why, when, how...等。特殊疑問詞後接一般疑問句，即倒裝語序；但如果特殊疑問詞在句中作主詞或修飾主詞，則後面與直述句語序一樣。

例：What are they doing in the lab?
他們在實驗室裡做什麼呢？（倒裝語序）
When do you go to school every day?
你每天什麼時間去上學？（倒裝語序）
How is the weather? 天氣怎麼樣？（倒裝語序）
Who will teach us English this term?
這個學期誰會教我們英文？（自然語序）

3.選擇疑問句

選擇疑問句是提出兩個或兩個以上答案來供對方選擇。它有以下兩種結構：

★ 一般疑問句＋or＋一般疑問句？

需要注意的是，or之後的一般疑問句和or之前的一般疑問句，兩者相同的部分通常被省略。

例：Would you like coffee or (would you like) juice?
你喜歡咖啡還是果汁？

★ 特殊疑問句，A or B?

例：Which do you prefer, talk show or soap opera?
你較喜歡哪一類，脫口秀還是肥皂劇？

4.反意疑問句

常用於口頭表達，用來提出意見或看法，詢問對方同意與否。反意疑問句由兩部分構成，前一部分是直述句形式，後一部分是附加的簡短問句形式。兩部分時態要一致。

需要注意的是，如果前一部分是肯定形式，後一部分要用否定形式；如果前一部分是否定形式，後一部分要用肯定形式。而且，回答時與中文的回答方式相當不一樣。

例：William is an exchange student, isn't he?
威廉是一名交換學生，是嗎？
We have no classes today, do we? 我們今天沒有課，對吧？

Level **3**

unless...

我們常說的「除非……」，含有交換條件的意味，在英文裡就是用這個句型來表達，例如：「除非你答應不說出去，我才要告訴你這個秘密。」

 關鍵句型 **點**

❶ unless 具有否定意義，常譯為「除非……」，「如果不……就不……」。unless 在意思上比較接近 if...not，所以兩者常可交替使用，只是 unless 的語氣比 if... not 重。但也不是所有情況下，unless 都可以與 if... not 互換。

例 You will fail the exam **unless** you study harder.
= **If** you **don't** study harder, you will fail the exam.
→除非你更加用功，否則你考試將會不及格。

❷ 如果unless引導的子句本身是否定形式，unless就不能由if...not所替代。

例 Don't consult a dictionary **unless** you really don't understand the word.
→除非你確實不懂那個字的意思，不然不要查字典。

會話演練 線

A I'm afraid I will not pass the exam next month.

B You will fail the exam **unless** you study harder.

A: 我恐怕考不過下個月的考試。

B: 除非你更加用功，否則你考試將會不及格。

A Why not go to the party with us?

B I will not go to the party **unless** he invites me.

A: 何不和我們一起去派對呢？

B: 除非他邀請我，否則我就不去參加派對。

A Can I consult a dictionary when I read this passage?

B Don't consult a dictionary **unless** you really don't understand the word.

A: 我閱讀這段文章時能查字典嗎？

B: 除非你確實不懂那個字的意思，不然不要查字典。

A Do you want to enter the singing contest?

B No, **unless** you want to sing a duet with me.

A: 你想參加歌唱比賽嗎？

B: 不要，除非你想跟我對唱。

Level

3

unless...

例句 **一連發**

❶ Unless the rain stops, we will not go out for flying a kite.
= **If** the rain **doesn't** stop, we will not go out for flying a kite.
除非雨停了，不然我們就不出去放風箏了。

❷ Don't ask me to explain **unless** you really don't understand.
除非你真的不懂，不然別叫我解釋。

❸ I can't finish it myself **unless** you help me.
除非你幫助我，不然我無法自己完成它。

❹ Unless I visit every bookstore in town, I will not know whether I can get the book I want.
如果我不到城裡每一家書店去看看，我就不知道是否能買到我想要的書。

❺ You will never get anywhere **unless** you have set your goal.
如果你不設定目標，你哪裡也去不了。

❻ This baby seldom cries **unless** he is hungry.
這個嬰兒除非是餓了，否則很少哭。

❼ They couldn't afford to live in such an expensive apartment **unless** they were rich.
除非他們很富有，否則就住不起這麼昂貴的公寓。

小小試身手

( ) **①** _____ he comes, we won't be able to go.
(A) Without
(B) Unless
(C) Except
(D) Even

( ) **②** They couldn't have arrived at the site instantly unless the police _____ a helicopter.
(A) had had
(B) had
(C) has
(D) could have

( ) **③** –I don't want to go to the party unless Alice will be there.
–_____
(A) Why do you hate Alice?
(B) She said she will go.
(C) Is Alice having a party?
(D) If Alice goes, I won't go either.

Level

3

unless...

Answer: **B、A、B**

① 句子意思是「除非他來，不然我們不能去。」not...unless 句型意思為「除非……才……」或「只有……才」。unless 引導的子句也可以放在句首，所以答案選 (B)。

② 句子意思是「除非警方有直升機，不然他們就無法立即趕到事發地點。」not...unless 句型意為「除非……才……」或「只有……才」。本題的 unless 子句表示了與過去事實相反的情況，所以要用過去的虛擬語氣形式：had ＋過去分詞，所以答案選 (A)。

③ 句子的意思是：「我不想去派對，除非愛麗絲會去。」「她有說她會去。」如果看懂了第一句，就知道説話者對愛麗絲並不討厭，還蠻願意在派對上見到她，因此答者應該不會回答 (A)「你幹嘛討厭愛麗絲？」或 (D)「如果她去，那我也不去。」而 (C) 天外飛來一筆，不符合對話邏輯，只有 (B) 為正確答案。

whether... or...

中文裡所說的「無論你要走還是要留，我都支持你」或「不管你答不答應，我都要這麼做」，都可以用這個句型來表達。

 關鍵句型 **點**

❶ 句型 Whether ...or... 意為「無論……還是……」，它可以用於引出正反、對錯等的兩種概念，是一種強烈的讓步語氣，即不管情況如何，正反兩方面都估計在內，總之，不會影響後面主句動作的結果。

例 **Whether** you like **or** dislike the job, you have to finish it.
→無論你喜歡還是不喜歡這個工作，你都必須完成它。

❷ 在whether...or...結構中，or不可省略，也不能用if來取代whether。whether...or...後面可以接不定詞、形容詞或其他片語。

例 **Whether** happy **or** sad, she always tries to keep smiling.
→不管開心還是難過，她總是試著保持微笑。

會話演練 線

A I wonder **whether** we should stay **or** go.

B It depends on you.

A: 我不知道我們是去還是留。

B: 由你來決定。

A I'm tired of the job of painting the house.

B **Whether** you like **or** dislike the job, you have to finish it.

A: 我厭倦了這個房子的粉刷工作。

B: 無論你喜歡還是不喜歡這個工作,你都必須做完它。

A **Whether** happy **or** sad, she always tries to keep smiling.

B What an optimistic girl she is!

A: 不管是開心還是難過,她總是試著保持微笑。

B: 她真是個樂觀的女孩!

A I don't care **whether** he likes these plants **or not**.

B Agreed. It's your garden, not his.

A: 我不在乎他喜不喜歡這些植物。

B: 我同意,這是你的花園,又不是他的。

Level

3

whether... or...

135

例句 **一連發**

❶ We don't know **whether** he will succeed **or** fail.
我們不知道他會成功，還是會失敗。

❷ **Whether** by accident **or** design, they met and fell in love.
無論是巧合還是有意安排，反正他們相遇而且相愛了。

❸ **Whether** you are a boy **or** a girl, I don't care.
無論你是男孩還是女孩，我不在乎。

❹ I don't care **whether** he is Swedish **or** Danish.
我不在乎他是瑞典人還是丹麥人。

❺ I believe in the dignity of labor, **whether** with head **or** hand.
我相信無論體力勞動還是腦力勞動都是高尚的。

❻ **Whether** right **or** wrong, he always gets the upper hand during debates.
無論是對還是錯，他總是在辯論中占上風。

❼ **Whether** money may bring us happiness **or** evil depends on how we get it and how we use it.
金錢帶給我們的是幸福還是邪惡取決於我們取得和使用金錢的方式。

( ) ❶ –Dad, I've finished my assignment.
　　 –Good, and _____ you play or watch TV, you mustn't disturb me.
　　 (A) whenever　　　　(B) whether
　　 (C) whatever　　　　(D) no matter

( ) ❷ She is always cheerful, _____ at home _____ at school.
　　 (A) whether / or　　　(B) X / and
　　 (C) X / or　　　　　(D) either / or

( ) ❸ It doesn't matter _____.
　　 (A) whether who wins or not
　　 (B) whether who wins
　　 (C) whether we win or not
　　 (D) whether or not we wins

Answer: **B、A、C**

❶ 句子意思是「爸爸，我寫完作業了。」「很好，不管你是玩還是看電視，不許打擾我。」whenever 的意思是「無論何時」，whatever 意思是「無論什麼」，no matter 後面要接疑問字，也表示「無論……」，意思都不符合題目，而且這三個選項都不需要和 or 搭配。Whether 可以和 or 搭配構成句型 Whether...or...，意思是「無論……還是……」，所以答案選 (B)。

❷ 句子意思是「無論是在家還是在學校，她總是興高采烈。」根據 she is always cheerful 和後面的 at home、at school，可以推斷逗號後面是用來說明前一句的內容：她是在兩方面都快樂。選項裡只有 whether...or... 有「無論……還是……」、「是……還是……」的意思，所以答案選 (A)。

❸ 句子的意思是：「無論我們獲勝與否都沒關係。」，(C) 為正確答案。(D) 不正確是因為動詞 wins 和名詞 we 搭配不起來，而 (A) 和 (B) 一次出現了太多不確定的因素，不只問了「有沒有贏」，還問了「誰贏」，在此種句型中一次只能選一件事情問，所以只有 (C) 正確。

Unit 03

What/How...!

當我們想要感嘆某個人或某件事情時，會說「多美的景色呀！」或「真是愚蠢的行為啊！」便可以用這個句型來表達。

關鍵句型 點

❶ what 後面要接名詞，當該名詞為可數名詞單數時，要在 what 後加上冠詞 a/an，形容詞只是用來進一步修飾名詞的。what 引導的感嘆句句型結構大致上有以下幾種：

What＋a/an＋（形容詞）＋可數名詞＋（主詞＋動詞）！

 What a clever boy he is! →他真是一個聰明的孩子啊！

What ＋（形容詞）＋不可數名詞＋（主詞＋動詞）！

 What nonsense he is talking! →他真是在胡說八道！

在 what 引導的感嘆句中，主詞和述部是正常語序，有時可以省略。

❷ how在此為副詞，用來修飾形容詞和副詞。how引導的感嘆句句型結構大致上有以下幾種：

How＋形容詞＋ a/an＋可數名詞單數＋主詞＋述語！

 How clever a boy he is! →他真是一個聰明的孩子啊！

How ＋形容詞＋主詞＋動詞！

 How crazy his plan seems! →他的計畫看起來好瘋狂！

How ＋副詞＋主詞＋動詞！

 How well Jane can skate! →珍溜冰溜得多好啊！

會話演練

A Tony got the first prize again in the contest.

B **What** a clever boy he is!/ **How** clever a boy he is!

A: 東尼在這次競賽中又獲得了第一名。

B: 他真是一個聰明的孩子啊！

A He is sharing his experiences in the US with the girls.

B **What** nonsense he is talking!

A: 他正在和那些女孩分享他在美國的經歷。

B: 他真是在胡說八道！

A **How** crazy his plan seems!

B I don't think so. I admire his courage very much.

A: 他的計畫看起來太瘋狂了！

B: 我不這麼認為。我很佩服他的勇氣。

A **How** well Jane can skate!

B She has been skating for five years.

A: 珍溜冰溜得多好啊！

B: 她溜冰已經五年了。

A **What** a sunny day!

B The forecast says it's going to rain in the afternoon though.

A: 今天天氣真好！

B: 但氣象預報說下午會下雨。

例句**一連發**

❶ What a great pity you missed the lecture again!
你又錯過了講座，真是太遺憾了！

❷ What a genius he is!
他真是個天才！

❸ What heavy snow it is!
好大的雪啊！

❹ What delicious cakes (they are)!
多好吃的蛋糕呀！

❺ What wonderful ideas (they are)!
多棒的主意啊！

❻ How great a building it is!
=**What** a great building it is!
多麼宏偉的建築啊！

❼ How lovely a baby she was!
=**What** a lovely baby she was!
她是個多麼可愛的寶寶啊！

❽ How sad your mother looks!
你媽媽看起來多傷心啊！

❾ How fluently she speaks English!
她英文說得多流利啊！

❿ How interesting (it is)!
多有趣啊！

⓫ How time flies!
真是時光飛逝！

小小**試身手**

( )❶ ____ food you've cooked!
(A) How a nice   (B) What a nice
(C) How nice   (D) What nice

( )❷ ____ terrible weather we've been having these days!
(A) What   (B) What a
(C) How   (D) How a

( )❸ What _____ salad!
(A) amazing
(B) an amazing
(C) amazing a
(D) amazing an

Answer: **D、A、B**

❶ 句子意思是「你做的東西太好吃了。」food 為不可數名詞，因此前面不能用冠詞 a。由於 how 修飾形容詞、副詞；what 修飾名詞。當修飾可數名詞單數時，how 和 what 引導的感嘆句可以互換，即：「What ＋ a/an ＋（形容詞）＋可數名詞單數＋主詞＋述部！」相當於「How ＋形容詞＋ a/an ＋可數名詞單數＋主詞＋述部！」而「How ＋形容詞＋不可數名詞」並不存在，因此只有 (D) 正確，其句型為「What ＋形容詞＋不可數名詞」。

❷ 句子意思是「這幾天的天氣真糟糕啊！」weather 為不可數名詞，因此前面不能用冠詞 a。選項 (C) 是 How ＋形容詞，後面不應有不可數名詞 weather。只有 (A) 符合句型「What ＋形容詞＋不可數名詞」。故正確選項為 (A)。

❸ 句子的意思是：「真是碗好讚的沙拉！」此句型為 What + 冠詞 + 形容詞 + 名詞，因此 (B) 為正確答案。

Unit 04 Do/Would you mind...?

中文裡所說的「你介意……？」例如——「你介意我抽煙嗎？」或「你介意我們換個話題嗎？」，表示委婉地詢問對方的意見，便可以用這個句型。

關鍵句型 點

❶ 當你想做某件事，但這件事可能會妨礙到別人，你可以用這個句型問對方以徵求意見。mind 後可以接動名詞或名詞，也可接子句。Do/Would you mind doing sth.? 常譯為「可否請你做……」這個句型多用 Would 開頭，用 Do 的情況較少。

 Do you mind my smoking here?

→你介意我在這裡抽煙嗎？

❷ 回答時，你如果同意或不反對別人做某事，答案用否定形式，經常會用的是 Certainly not. / Of course not. 等，意思是「我不介意」；而如果你不同意別人做某事，答案則要用肯定形式，一般會用 I am sorry... 或 I'm afraid... 等緩和語氣，來婉轉拒絕；或說 I'd rather you wouldn't. / I wish you wouldn't.。

 -**Would you mind** looking after my cat?

→你介意照顧一下我的貓咪嗎？

– Not at all. I'd be happy to. →一點也不介意，我很樂意。

會話演練

A **Do you mind** if I open the windows and the door?

B Certainly not./Of course not.

A: 你介意我把窗戶和門都打開嗎？

B: 當然不介意。

A **Would you mind** if I turn up the TV a bit?

B Yes, I do, because I'm doing my homework now.

A: 你介意我把電視機音量調大一點嗎？

B: 我介意，因為我現在正在寫作業。

A **Do you mind** my smoking here?

B I'm sorry, but I do.

A: 你介意我在這裡抽煙嗎？

B: 對不起，我介意。

A I'll be away on a business trip. **Would you mind** looking after my cat?

B Not at all. I'd be happy to.

A: 我要去出差。你介意照顧一下我的貓咪嗎？

B: 一點也不介意，我很樂意。

A **Would you mind if** I take a cookie?

B Go ahead, help yourself.

A: 你介意我拿走一塊餅乾嗎？

B: 盡量拿，沒問題。

Level

3

Do/Would you mind...?

例句 **一連發**

❶ Do you mind if I turn on the radio?
你介意我開收音機嗎？

❷ Would you mind making some room for the patient?
你可以替這位病人挪點位置出來嗎？

❸ Do you mind if I tell him your secret?
你介意我把你的秘密告訴他嗎？

❹ Would you mind my moving your car forward?
我把你的車往前移動一下，你介意嗎？

❺ Would you mind if I play the drums in the room next door?
你介意我在隔壁房間打鼓嗎？

❻ Do you mind singing a song for me?
你可以為我唱首歌嗎？

❼ Would you mind if she came here late?
如果她晚到，你會介意嗎？

❽ Would you mind if I talk to you later?
如果我晚一點再跟你談，你介意嗎？

小小試身手

( ) ❶ –Do you mind if ____ here?
　　　 –Of course not, help yourself.
　　　 (A) sitting　　　　　　　(B) my sitting
　　　 (C) I sitting　　　　　　(D) I sit

( ) ❷ –It's so cold here. Would you mind my closing the
　　　　window?
　　　 –____.
　　　 (A) No, you can't　　　　(B) Yes, you can
　　　 (C) Of course not　　　　(D) Yes, I mind

( ) ❸ –Do you mind if I play the piano?
　　　 –_____
　　　 (A) No, it's fine with me.　　(B) Yes, play it.
　　　 (C) No, I do.　　　　　　　(D) Yes, I will play.

Answer: **D、C、A**

❶ 句子意思是「你介不介意我坐在這裡？」「不，你請坐吧。」
Do you mind if...? 這個句型中，if 後面可以接子句。千萬不要
把它與句型 Do you mind (one's) doing ...? 混淆。If 子句中要有
主詞和述部，所以答案為 (D)。

❷ 句子意思是：「這裡太冷了。你介意我把窗戶關上嗎？」「當
然不介意。」關於 Would you mind (one's) doing...? 的回答方
式，你如果同意或不反對別人做某事，答案用否定形式，也可
直接先說 No，然後再根據問句內容回答。(A) 選項的 No 後面
接 you can't 就完全誤解了 no 在這裡的含義，no 在這裡表示「不
介意」的意思，後面說 you can't（你不能關窗戶）就和前面意
思矛盾了，所以排除 (A)。Of course not. 表示「當然不介意」，
所以答案為 (C)。

❸ 句子的意思是：「你介意我彈鋼琴嗎？」「沒問題，我不介意。」
若回答 Yes 表達會介意，若回答 No，則表達不介意，因此 (B)、
(C)、(D) 均產生意思上的衝突（(B) 我介意，請彈吧、(C) 不介
意，我介意、(D) 我介意，我來彈），因此只有 (A) 為正確答案。

145

It＋adj.＋of/for sb.＋to v. ...

　　「這件事對你而言應該輕而易舉」以及「你真是太聰明了，竟然想到這個好主意」，這兩句話都可以用這個句型，但其中一個句子裡會用到 of，另一個句子裡會用到 for，但究竟哪個句子該用哪個字呢？只要看完這個單元，這個問題對你而言就輕而易舉了！

關鍵句型 點

❶ It's＋adj.＋of/for sb. to do sth.是一個常見的句型，常翻譯成「對某人來説，做某事是……。」句首的it是形式主詞，後面的不定詞才是真正的主詞。另外，需要特別注意介系詞的使用。這個句型中要用of還是for取決於前面的形容詞。

❷ 若形容詞表示的是人的特質、性格（如：brave, careful, foolish, good, kind, nice, clever, stupid, wise...），需用of。

例 **It's** stupid **of** you **to** have such an idea.
　　→你有種想法真是太愚蠢了。

　　It's very kind **of** you **to** do so. →你這麼做真是太好了。

❸ 若形容詞只是對動作的一般性描述（如：difficult, dangerous, important...），則用for。

例 **It's** very easy **for** him **to** pass the exam.
　　→對他來説通過這次考試太容易了。

會話演練

A He hasn't reviewed the lesson at all.

B Don't worry. **It's** very easy **for** him **to** pass the exam.

A: 他完全沒有復習這個單元。

B: 別擔心，對他來說通過這次考試太容易了。

A I have decided to quit school.

B Oh, no! **It's** stupid **of** you **to** have such an idea.

A: 我決定退學。

B: 哦，不！你有種想法真是太愚蠢了。

A You can stay in my house during the summer vacation.

B **It's** very kind **of** you **to** offer this.

A: 暑假期間你可以住在我家。

B: 你願意這麼做真是太好了。

A I baked you a cake.

B **It's** very nice **of** you **to** have done so.

A: 我烤了一個蛋糕給你。

B: 你這樣做，真是太好了。

Level

3

It + adj. + of/for sb. + to v. ...

例句 **一連發**

❶ It's important **for** us to learn English well.
對我們來說學好英文很重要。

❷ It's very nice **of** you to give me two tickets for the World Cup.
你給了我兩張世界盃的票，真是太好了。

❸ This sign means that **it is** dangerous **for** anybody to walk on the ice.
這個標誌的意思是，任何人在冰上行走都是危險的。

❹ It's nice **of** you to say so.
你這樣說真是太好了。

❺ It's very difficult **for** us to finish the job in two days.
在兩天內就完成這項工作對我們來說很困難。

❻ It's wise **of** him to give up the decision.
他放棄這個決定是明智的。

❼ It's not safe **for** anyone to swim in this river.
對任何人來說，在這河裡游泳都不安全。

小小試身手

( ) **❶** It's very nice _____ you to take care of my baby while I was on holiday.
    (A) of   (B) with
    (C) to   (D) for

( ) **❷** It is dangerous _____ children to play with fire.
    (A) of   (B) for
    (C) with   (D) that

( ) **❸** It was very _____ him to have made this mistake.
    (A) stupid of   (B) nice for
    (C) easy of   (D) smart for

Answer: **A**、**B**、**A**

❶ 句子意思是:「你在我去度假時替我照顧我的寶寶,你真是太好了。」這是一個對別人表示讚美的句型。這裡用的是 It is + adj. + of/for + sb. to v.... 句型。應該選 of 還是 for,主要是看結構中 of 和 for 前面的那個形容詞能不能直接修飾 you。如果可以,就表示形容詞是形容人本身的特質、性格等,即用 of;否則就是對動作的一般性描述,用 for。很顯然,根據句意可知,這裡的形容詞 nice 修飾形容的是 you,故選 (A)。

❷ 句子意思是:「對小孩來說玩火是危險的。」It is + adj. + of/for + sb. to v.... 是固定句型,根據句子意思可判斷,其中的形容詞 dangerous 是用來描述孩子玩火的這個行為,而不是形容孩子本身的特質,所以介系詞要用 for,答案選 (B)。

❸ 句子的意思是:「他犯了這個錯真是愚蠢。」使用了前面所提的 It's + V + of sb. to...,表示他犯這個錯誤很蠢,選 (A) 為正確答案。若要表達「對他來說很容易就會犯這個錯誤了」,需用 easy for 而不是 easy of,因此 (C) 是不對的。

Unit 06 I don't think/believe/ suppose that ...

「我認為這個消息是不正確的」或「我相信這個消息是不正確的」或「我猜這個消息是不正確的」等，都表達了自己對某件事的否定看法，便適合用這個句型。

 關鍵句型 點

❶ 這是由動詞 think, believe, suppose, expect, fancy, imagine 後接子句所構成的否定轉移句型。如果主句的動詞是 think, believe, suppose, expect, fancy, imagine 等表示心理活動的動詞時，其後面子句的否定詞 not 通常轉移到主句中，成為「形式否定主句，意義否定子句」，即主句的動詞用否定式，而子句的動詞用肯定式。其中的 that 可以省略。

例 **We don't believe that** he can translate this book.
→我們認為他翻譯不出這本書。

❷ 需要強調的是，當 think 用在疑問句中時，一般不要求否定轉移；動詞 hope 也不可進行否定轉移。

例 **Do you think** my mother wouldn't permit this?
→你認為我媽媽不會答應嗎？

會話演練

會話翻譯

A **I don't think** she's at home, but I'll go and see.

B You are wasting time.

A: 我認為她不在家,但我會去看看。

B: 你是在浪費時間。

A **We don't believe that** he can translate this book.

B Why do you think so?

A: 我們認為他翻譯不出這本書。

B: 你們為什麼這麼認為?

A I want to invite Bonnie to see the movie with me.

B **I don't imagine that** she'll enjoy it.

A: 我想邀邦妮和我去看那部電影。

B: 我猜想她不會喜歡這部電影。

A Come on! Don't let your mother know.

B **Do you think** my mother wouldn't permit this?

A: 算了吧!別讓你媽媽知道這件事了。

B: 你認為我媽媽不會答應嗎?

A **I don't expect** to see him here.

B Why not? He lives here!

A: 我沒預期到會在這裡見到他。

B: 為什麼?他住在這裡耶!

例句 **一連發**

❶ I don't think he will come this afternoon.
我認為他今天下午不會來。

❷ I don't suppose that they have got married.
我猜他們還沒有結婚。

❸ I don't imagine that you would not do anything.
我猜想你不會什麼都不做。

❹ We don't expect they have finished the work.
我們預期他們還沒有完成工作。

❺ I don't suppose he will return to his hometown after a few years of studying abroad.
我猜想他在國外學習幾年後不會回家鄉了。

❻ I don't think there is anything interesting in your pictures.
我認為你的畫沒有什麼有趣的地方。

❼ We don't imagine taxes will be reduced this year.
我們猜今年稅收不會減少。

( ) ❶ –I will ask Jerry to help me do my homework.
　　 –I ＿＿ think it ＿＿ a good idea.
　　 (A) X / be 　　　　　　(B) X / isn't
　　 (C) don't / isn't 　　　(D) don't / is

( ) ❷ ＿＿ don't imagine they ＿＿ married.
　　 (A) I / X 　　　　　　　(B) I / are
　　 (C) They / X 　　　　　(D) They / be

( ) ❸ I ＿＿＿＿＿ that you would be here so soon.
　　 (A) don't imagined
　　 (B) don't suppose
　　 (C) didn't expect
　　 (D) hadn't guess

Answer: **D、B、C**

❶ 句子意思是「我要請傑瑞幫我做作業。」「我認為這不是個好主意。」這裡用的是否定轉移句型 I don't think...。要表達「認為……不是……」，就要用否定轉移句型，將 think 後面子句的否定詞 not 轉移到主句中，所以選 (D)。

❷ 句子意思是「我猜他們沒有結婚。」這裡用的是否定轉移句型 I don't think...。否定轉移句型的主詞一般是第一人稱 I 和 We，其次，They married 的說法是不對的，be married 才可以表示結婚的狀態，所以選 (B)。

❸ 句子的意思是：「我沒預期到你會這麼早到。」由於對方一定是已經到了，說話者才會說出「沒預期到……」（要是對方根本還沒到，那就符合說話者的預期），因此以現在式出現的 (A) 和 (B) 不對。(D) 的 guess 需改為 guessed 才符合文法，只有 (C) 為正確答案。

Unit 07 It's time (for sb.) to do sth....

我們常說的「該是睡覺的時候了」或「該出去走走了」，表示做某件事的時機成熟，便可以用這個句型。

 關鍵句型 **點**

❶ It's time for sb. to do sth. 是一個常見的句型。意思是「該是某人做……的時候了」。當然也可以說 It's time to do sth.，意思是「該是做……的時候了。」It 為虛主詞，無實際意義，句子的真正主詞是 to do sth.。

例 **It's time for** us **to** go home.
　→該是我們回家的時候了。

❷ It's time for sb. to do sth.還可以用句型「It's time for sth.」來替換，後者的意思也是「到了……的時間了」、「是……的時候了」。需要注意的是for後面要直接接名詞或代名詞。

例 **It's time for** school.
　→該上學去了。
　It's time for a snack.
　→該吃點心了。

會話演練 **線**

會話翻譯

A It's five o'clock now. **It's time for** us **to** go home.

B It's too early. Let's play basketball for an hour.

A: 現在五點了。該是我們回家的時候了。

B: 太早了。讓我們打一個小時籃球吧！

A Be quick. **It's time for** school.

B But I haven't had breakfast yet.

A: 快點！該上學去了。

B: 但是我還沒吃早餐。

A Your hair is too long. **It's time for** you **to** have a haircut.

B I don't like to cut my hair short.

A: 你的頭髮太長了，該剪頭髮了。

B: 我不喜歡把頭髮剪短。

A Why not study in your room, Charlie?

B **It's time for** me **to** relax.

A: 查理，為什麼不在你房間裡讀書？

B: 我該放鬆一下了。

It's time (for sb.) to do sth....

例句 **一連發**

❶ It's time for you **to** clean the classroom.
該是你打掃教室的時候了。

❷ It's time to buy some milk.
該去買些牛奶了。

❸ Come on. **It's time** to have supper.
快來啊！該吃晚餐了。

❹ It's no use envying others' success. **It's time for** you **to** work hard.
羨慕別人的成功是沒有用的，該是你努力工作的時候了。

❺ I think **it's time for** us **to** start the lesson now.
我想現在是我們開始上課的時候了。

❻ Hurry up; **it's time for** class.
快點，該上課了。

❼ It's time to think about your future.
該是思考你的未來的時候了。

❽ It's time to order pizza.
是時候該叫披薩了。

( )❶ It's time _____ us _____ a meeting.
(A) for / to have　　　(B) of / to have
(C) for / X　　　　　(D) to / to have

( )❷ –Hurry up. It's time _____ homework.
–May I watch TV a little longer?
(A) of　　　　　　　(B) for
(C) to　　　　　　　(D) with

( )❸ It's time _____ go home.
(A) to　　　　　　　(B) for us to
(C) for us　　　　　(D) to us for

Answer: **A**、**B**、**B**

❶ 句子意思是「我們開會的時間到了。」句型 It's time for sb. to do sth. 中，it 是虛主詞，真正的主詞是後面的不定詞 to have a meeting。如果需要說明是「某人」做某事的時間，則需要再用介系詞 for，所以選 (A)。

❷ 句子意思是「快點！該寫作業了。」「我可以再多看一會電視嗎？」It's time for sth. 是固定句型。根據句子上下文意思可猜想應該是家長和孩子之間的對話，實際上完整的意思可以表達為：It's time for you to do your homework. 但是這裡的選項裡沒有 for sb. to do 的結構，只有名詞 homework，所以這裡應該用介系詞 for，後面直接可以接 homework，故選 (B)。

❸ 句子的意思是：「是時候我們該回家了。」此處使用的是「It's time for sb. to + 原 V」句型，選擇 (B) 為正確答案。

by the time...

　　「到了明年，我們就可以實現夢想了」或「等你回來的時候，我們再好好聊聊」，都是表達到了某個時間點就會發生某件事，這時便可以用這個句型。

關鍵句型 **點**

❶ by the time (that)的意思是「等到……時」，後面接時間子句，that可以省略。

❷ 如果子句中的動詞是用過去簡單式，主句的動詞就用過去完成式。

例 **By the time** I got to the airport, the plane had taken off.
→我到機場時，飛機已經起飛了。

❸ 如果子句的動詞用現在簡單式，主句的動詞就用未來完成式。

例 **By the time** you come to see me, I will have recovered myself. →你來看我的時候，我就會痊癒的。

會話演練 線

A **By the time** I got to the airport, the plane had taken off.

B You should have set out earlier.

A: 我到機場時，飛機已經起飛了。

B: 你應該早點出門的。

A I will come to see you again next week.

B **By the time** you come to see me, I will have recovered myself.

A: 我下星期再來看你。

B: 你來看我的時候，我就會痊癒的。

A **By the time** he was ten years old, he had learned English and French all by himself.

B What a genius!

A: 到十歲的時候，他已經自學了英文和法文。

B: 他真是個天才。

A Where's everyone?

B I have no idea. **By the time** I got here, this whole place was empty.

A: 大家都去哪了？

B: 我也不知道。我到這裡的時候，這裡就已經空空如也了。

例句**一連發**

❶ **By the time** he called me, I had finished this article.
他打電話給我時，我已經寫完那篇文章了。

❷ **By the time** you come home next time, the new house will have been built.
下次你回家的時候，新房子就建好了。

❸ The truck will have arrived **by the time** you have all the things packed up.
等你把所有東西都打包好時，卡車就會抵達了。

❹ **By the time** you arrive in London, we will have stayed in Europe for two weeks.
等你到倫敦時，我們就已經在歐洲待兩週了。

❺ I shall have finished my work **by the time** you return.
在你回來時，我應該已經把工作完成了。

❻ **By the time** your son was born, my daughter had graduated from high school.
你兒子出生時，我的女兒已經高中畢業了。

❼ **By the time** I got there, they had ended the meeting.
我到那裡時，他們已經開完會了。

小小試身手

( ) ❶ By the time you receive this letter, I _____ this city for my home town.
(A) have left   (B) will have left
(C) leave   (D) will leave

( ) ❷ By the time she got home, her mother _____ for Taipei to attend a meeting.
(A) will leave   (B) leaves
(C) will have left   (D) had left

( ) ❸ By the time he woke up, _____.
(A) the house was in flames.
(B) I will be in Japan.
(C) she eats the whole cake.
(D) the ring is stolen.

Answer: **B、D、A**

❶ 這個句子的意思是「等到你收到這封信時，我已經離開這座城市回我的家鄉了。」「by the time (that) ＋時間子句＋主句」這個句型中的主句要用完成式，但應該用過去完成式還是未來完成式，主要是看 by the time 後面引導的時間子句的時間點發生在過去、現在或未來。本題中的 you receive this letter 是現在式，所以主句時態應該用未來完成式。正確答案是 (B)。

❷ 這個句子的意思是「等到她回家時，她媽媽已經去台北開會了。」by the time 引導的時間子句的時間點發生在過去，所以主句時態應該用過去完成式。正確答案是 (D)。

❸ 句子的意思是：「等到他醒來的時候，房子已經著火了。」由 woke 為過去式可判斷此處講述的是過去發生的事，因此選擇唯一的過去式選項 (A) 為正確答案。

❶ What _____ house it is!

(A) beautiful a

(B) a beautiful

(C) beautiful an

(D) an beautiful

❷ _____ strong _____ !

(A) What / is he

(B) What / he is

(C) How / is he

(D) How / he is

❸ Would you mind _____ next to you?

(A) to sit

(B) that I sit

(C) if I sit

(D) whether I sit

❹ –Do you mind sending me one of these stamps?

–_____.

(A) No, you can't

(B) Yes, you can

(C) Certainly not

(D) Yes, I don't mind

❺ _____ himself wrong, but also his friends were wrong.

(A) Not was only he

(B) Not only he

(C) Not only was he

(D) Not only was

6 – Can't you see anything?

– _____, I can't see _____.

(A) No / nothing   (B) No / anything

(C) Yes / nothing   (D) Yes / anything

7 You will never succeed _____ you study hard.

(A) unless   (B) if

(C) though   (D) when

過
關
大
挑
戰

8 It's bad _____ you _____ so much wine.

(A) about / drinking   (B) of / to drink

(C) for / to drink   (D) with / to drink

9 _____ he drives or takes the train, he'll be here on time.

(A) What   (B) Although

(C) If   (D) Whether

10 I don't think they _____ if it rains heavily.

(A) will come   (B) will not come

(C) comes   (D) don't come

❶ 這是個典型的感嘆句，其中的house是可數名詞單數。當修飾可數名詞單數時，how和what引導的感嘆句可以互換，即：「What＋a/an＋（形容詞）＋可數名詞單數＋主詞＋述部!」相當於「How＋形容詞＋ a/an＋可數名詞單數＋主詞＋述部！」本句句首是what，所以後面要接「a/an＋形容詞」。但是beautiful的開頭字母不是母音，所以冠詞要用a，答案選(B)。

❷ what是用來修飾後面的名詞。這個題目中修飾的是形容詞strong，所以不適合用what。而how在感嘆句中是副詞，用來修飾形容詞和副詞。形容詞的作用是描述後面主詞的狀態，副詞的作用則是修飾後面的述部，句型結構是：「How＋形容詞／副詞＋主詞＋述部！」而且，主詞和述部不用倒裝，用正常語序，所以選(D)。

❸ Would you mind if I do...？是個固定句型，用來表示請求對方的許可，相當於Would you mind doing sth.?意思為「如果我做某事，你反對／介意嗎？」mind後面接子句時，前面要用if，不能改成that，也不能改成whether，所以選(C)。

❹ 回答Would you mind (one's) doing...?這個句型時，你如果同意或不反對別人做某事，答案用否定形式，也可直接先說用No，然後再根據問句內容回答，也可直接說No, I don't mind.或Certainly not. / Of course not. / Not at all. / No, go ahead.等，意思是「不，我不介意。」而如果你不同意或反對別人做某事，答案則要用肯定形式，可以說：Yes, I do.，但更常用的是語氣緩和客氣的I am sorry...或I'm afraid...等。所以選(C)。

❺ not only引導的那部分內容放在句首時，其後面的內容需要部分倒裝，即用was幫助構成倒裝，而but also及其引導的那部分內容語序保持不變，所以答案選(C)。

❻ 這裡要注意的是否定疑問句句型「Can't you...?」的回答形式。這種句型在回答時要注意避免受中文思維的影響。如果答案是肯定的，就用Yes，後面接相應的肯定結構；如果答案是否定的，就用No，後面接相應的否定結構。後句想要表達的是「我沒看見任何東西」，所以前面要用No，中文翻譯成「是的」。而 I can't see 前面有can't了，後面只能接anything，不能再接含有否定意味的nothing，所以選(B)。

7 if意為「如果」；though意為「儘管」；when意為「當……」；unless是具有否定意義的從屬連接詞，意為「如果……不……」、「除非……」。句子中因為有never，所以表示否定含義，相當於not...unless，可以翻譯為「你如果不努力學習，就永遠不會成功。」或「除非你努力學習，否則你永遠不會成功。」答案是(A)。

8 在It is＋adj.＋of/for＋sb. to do...的句型中，句子中的bad形容的不是you的特質、人品等，而是說明喝太多酒這件事的不好後果和影響，所以介系詞要用for，選(C)。

9 句型whether ...or ...用於引出正反、對錯等的兩種概念，是一種強烈的讓步語氣，即不管情況如何，正反兩方面都估計在內。總之，不會影響後面主句動作的結果，意思是「無論……還是……」雖然whether和if 在很多情況下可以互換，但是在這個句型中，不能用if來取代whether。答案是(D)。

10 本題的句子意思是「我認為如果下大雨，他們是不會來的。」這裡是否定轉移句型I don't think...，意思是「認為……不是……」。這個句子乍看之下比較複雜，但分析一下結構就可以發現：they will come if it rains heavily是由if引導的條件子句，表示將來的動作或情況，所以主句用未來式will come。而複合句they will come if it rains heavily又充當了I don't think的受詞，所以形式上主句中的not實際上是否定了will come。正確答案是(A)。

過關測驗解答

01~05: (B)(D)(C)(C)(C)　　　　　　　06~10: (B)(A)(C)(D)(A)

Level 3
補充文法面

please, let 的祈使句
what, how 的感嘆句

1 祈使句

祈使句是用來表示請求、命令、叮嚀、邀請、勸告、號召、祝願等的句子。

首先，需要瞭解的是，祈使句的主詞通常是第二人稱，且常被省略。當然，如果要加強語氣或為了明確指出請求、命令、邀請時，可以不省略主詞 you。其次，我們來看看祈使句的結構及其用法。

1. 一般祈使句的肯定形式：直接用原形動詞作述部，後接受詞、補語等。

例：Open your mouth, please.
　　請張開你的嘴。
　　Be quiet! 安靜！

2. 一般祈使句的否定形式：

★ do not (don't) ＋述部動詞
例：Don't worry. 不要擔心。

★ never ＋述部動詞
例：Never do such things.
　　絕對不要做這種事情。

★ no + V-ing

例：No smoking. 禁止吸煙。
No parking. 禁止停車。

3.let 祈使句的肯定式：

★ let me ＋原形動詞（讓我……）
例：Let me do it by myself. 讓我自己做這件事吧！

★ let us ＋原形動詞（讓我們……）
例：Let us forget it. 讓我們把這件事忘了吧！

★ let's ＋原形動詞（讓我們……）
例：Let's go on an outing. 我們去郊遊吧！

★ let ＋第三人稱單複數受詞＋原形動詞（讓……）
例：Let her go with us. 讓她和我們一起去吧！

let 開頭引導的祈使句，多表示建議或請求。尤其是「let us ＋原形動詞」和「let's ＋原形動詞」在口語表達中十分常見。但因為這兩個句型形似且很容易混淆，所以要特別注意它們的區別：let us（請讓我們……）的主詞是「你」，表示徵求對方許可，希望對方允許，但動作本身執行者並不包括對方；let's（讓我們……）的主詞是「我們」，表示提出建議或請求，希望對方一起執行，即動作本身包括說話者和聽話者兩方。

例：Let us help her. 請讓我們幫助她。（幫助者不包含「你」）
Let's help her. 讓我們來幫助她吧！（幫助者包含「你」）

4.let 祈使句的否定式：在 let 前面加 don't 或在原形動詞前加 not。
例：Don't let her play on the street. 不要讓她在街上玩耍。
Let's not say anything about it. 我們就別提到這件事了。

2▷感嘆句

感嘆句是用來表達説話時的強烈情感（例如：喜悦、憤怒、驚訝、厭惡、讚美等）的一種特殊句型。和中文一樣，英文中的感嘆句句尾也用感嘆號。英文感嘆句中最基本和最常見的是以 what 開頭的感嘆句句型和以 how 開頭的感嘆句句型兩種。what 和 how 與所修飾的詞放在句首，其他部分用直述句語序。

1.以what開頭的感嘆句：

★ What＋a(n)＋(形容詞)＋可數名詞單數＋(主詞＋述部)！

例：What a cute puppy (it is)!
　　好可愛的小狗啊！
　　What an honest girl (you are)!
　　妳真是個誠實的女孩！

★ What＋(形容詞)＋可數名詞複數＋(主詞＋述部)！

例：What beautiful flowers (they are)!
　　多漂亮的花啊！

★ What＋(形容詞)＋不可數名詞＋(主詞＋述部)！

例：What bad news (it is)!
　　真是個壞消息！

★ What＋主詞＋述部！

例：What Dad suffered in the past!
　　爸爸過去吃了多少苦啊！

2.以how開頭的感嘆句：

★ How＋形容詞＋主詞＋述部！

例：How moving the story is.
　　多感人的故事啊！

★ How＋副詞＋主詞＋述部！

例：How high he jumped!
　　他跳得多高啊！

★ How＋主詞＋述部！

例：How we miss you!
　　我們多麼想念你啊！

★How＋形容詞＋a(n)＋可數名詞單數＋主詞＋述部！

例：How brave a soldier he is!
　　他是多麼勇敢的士兵啊！

由此可以看出，what 是用來修飾名詞的，即使該名詞前還有其他的修飾成分，what 最終修飾的還是名詞。how 是用來修飾形容詞、副詞或動詞的。

當修飾的是可數名詞單數時，what 開頭的感嘆句可以跟 how 開頭的感嘆句互換，所表示的意義不變。

感嘆句在表示激動強烈的感情時，口語中常常採用省略句，其後面的主詞和述部往往可以省略。

除了以 what 開頭的感嘆句和以 how 開頭的感嘆句以外，還有幾種感嘆句在口語中也很常見：以感嘆詞或單個形容詞、副詞表示的感嘆句，如，Oh!（啊！哦！哎喲！）；Well!（好啦！）；Why!（豈有此理！）；Excellent!（好極了！）。以片語表示的感嘆句，如：Dear me!（哎呀！）My God!（天哪！）。

Level 4

I wish...

在許願時，我們常會說「希望……」、「但願……」或「祝你……」，這時，都可以用這個句型來表達，例如：「真希望你在這裡。」「但願這不是真的。」或「祝你佳節愉快。」等。

 關鍵句型 **點**

❶ 這個句型是一個使用虛擬語氣的典型句型。wish 後面接 that 子句，子句使用虛擬語氣表示某種不能實現的主觀願望，它們都與事實相反。that 經常被省略。此時，假設內容的時態都應比事實的時態往後退一步。

主要有以下三種形式：

· 表示對現在的願望：「wish ＋主詞＋過去式」

例 **I wish** I had one. →我真希望我有一個。

· 表示對過去的遺憾：「wish ＋主詞＋ had ＋過去分詞」或「would/could/might ＋ have ＋過去分詞」。

例 **I wish** I'd gone to bed earlier last night.
→我真希望昨天晚上我早一點上床睡覺。

· 表示對未來的願望：「wish ＋主詞＋ would/should/could/might ＋動詞原形」。

❷ wish自身的時態並不影響子句的動詞形式，所以如果將wish改為過去式wished，其後的that子句中的動詞形式不變。

❸ 另外，這個句型的主詞也可以是其他人稱。

例 **He wished** he hadn't met her. →他希望他沒有遇見她。

會話演練 線

會話翻譯

A Do you have a laptop?

B No, but **I wish** I had one.

A: 你有筆記型電腦嗎？

B: 沒有，但我真希望我有一台。

A I'm so sleepy. **I wish** I'd gone to bed earlier last night.

B Don't stay up late anymore.

A: 我睏死了。我真希望昨天晚上有早一點上床睡覺。

B: 以後不要再熬夜了。

A Emily left him and hurt him deeply.

B So **he wished** he hadn't met her.

A: 艾蜜麗離開了他並且深深地傷害了他。

B: 所以他希望他沒有遇見她。

A **I wish** I were super rich.

B Don't we all?

A: 我真希望我超有錢。

B: 我們不都這樣希望嗎？

A **I wish** I had a dog.

B Stop wishing and go adopt one then.

A: 我真希望我有一隻狗。

B: 別希望了，直接去領養一隻不就行了。

例句 **一連發**

❶ I wish (that) I had a better memory.
但願我的記性好一點。

❷ I wish it would stop raining.
但願雨能停止。

❸ I wish (that) I hadn't wasted so much time.
我真希望我沒有浪費掉這麼多時間。

❹ I wish you would be quiet.
我希望你安靜下來。

❺ I wished I hadn't spent so much time doing such meaningless things.
我要是那時沒有花那麼多時間做這種無意義的事情就好了。

❻ I wish that I knew something about gardening.
我希望我懂一點園藝就好了。

❼ I wish I would not be nervous next time.
我希望我下次不會再緊張。

❽ He wishes (that) he hadn't met her.
他真希望沒有遇見她。

❾ I wish that you would look younger and younger.
祝你外表越來越年輕。

小小 試身手

( ) ❶ I wish I _____ longer this morning, but I had to get up and came to class.
(A) could have slept   (B) slept
(C) might have slept   (D) have slept

( ) ❷ How I wish I_____ beautiful!
(A) were   (B) am
(C) will be   (D) should be

( ) ❸ I wish I _____, but all I have is a bike.
(A) had a bicycle   (B) had a car
(C) have a motorbike   (D) have two bikes

Answer: **A、A、B**

❶ 句子的意思是「我真希望今天早上我能多睡一會，但是我必須起床去上課。」在句型 I wish... 中，動詞 wish 後面接子句，動詞要用虛擬語氣。根據後半句中的動詞 had to 和整個句子的含義，可知說話者是在表達對過去的遺憾，這顯然是與過去事實相反的情況，所以要用「could + have + 過去分詞」，答案選 (A)。

❷ 句子意思是「我多希望長得漂亮！」wish 引導子句表示不能實現的主觀願望，要用虛擬語氣。依子句的意思和語氣來判斷，說話者可能長得不漂亮，所以她要表達想要漂亮的這個願望——這是在表達對自身現況的主觀願望，所以子句的 be 動詞應該用 were，答案選 (A)。

❸ 句子的意思是：「我真希望我有一台汽車，但我就只有一台腳踏車而已。」wish 後面的假設語氣需往回推一個時態，此處應使用過去式。而使用過去式的 (A) 與 (B) 中，由於說話者已經有腳踏車了，不需要希望自己有一台腳踏車，因此 (A) 不正確，必須選 (B)。

or/otherwise...

要提出警告時，我們會說：「你最好照我說的話去做，否則後果自行負責」或「你要自己振作起來，不然誰也幫不了你」，這時就可以用這個句型。

 關鍵句型 **點**

❶ 這是在口語表達和書面格式中都很適用的句型，記住它的結構是「祈使句＋or/otherwise＋陳述句」。它的意思相當於中文的「……，否則……」。前面的祈使句是條件，而後面的陳述句是結果。or和otherwise這兩個連接詞表示逆意的條件關係，即前面的條件和後面的結果不一致。or和otherwise前的祈使句常以逗號結尾，但有時也用句號。

例 Hurry up, **or** I'll be late. →快一點，要不然我要遲到了。

❷ 在這個句型中，前面也可以改成陳述句，即「陳述句＋or/otherwise＋陳述句」。

例 You must take the medicine, **otherwise** your cold will grow worse. →你必須吃藥，否則你的感冒會加重。

會話翻譯

A Hurry up, **or** I'll be late.

B Tough luck. My car has broken down.

A: 快一點，要不然我要遲到了。

B: 真倒楣，我的車拋錨了。

A I wish I had a big house.

B Work hard **or** you can't afford a big house in the future.

A: 但願我有一棟大房子。

B: 努力工作吧，不然你將來買不起大房子。

A Be there on time, **otherwise** you'll create a bad impression.

B Thank you for reminding me.

A: 要準時到，否則你會給人家留下不好的印象。

B: 謝謝你的提醒。

A I hate taking medicine.

B You must take the medicine, **otherwise** your cold will get worse.

A: 我討厭吃藥。

B: 你必須吃藥，否則你的感冒會加重。

例句 **一連發**

❶ Hurry up, **or** you won't catch the train.
　　快走，要不然你趕不上火車了。

❷ Put on your jacket, **or** you'll catch a cold.
　　穿上夾克，不然你會感冒的。

❸ Do it now, **otherwise** it will be too late.
　　馬上做，否則就太晚了。

❹ Listen to the teacher carefully, **or** you won't understand him.
　　專心聽講，否則你會聽不懂老師在説什麼。

❺ Work harder, **otherwise** you'll fail the exam.
　　要更用功，否則你會通不過考試。

❻ Don't eat so much, **or** you will put on weight quickly.
　　不要吃那麼多，不然你會很快變胖。

❼ Take a rest, **or** you'll be worn out.
　　休息一下，不然你會耗盡體力。

❽ Don't work so hard, **or** you'll get sick.
　　不要那麼辛苦，不然你會生病的。

小小試身手

( ) ❶ Go and see for yourself, _____ you will never believe me.
(A) when
(B) which
(C) or
(D) and

( ) ❷ Hands up, _____ I'll shoot.
(A) and
(B) so
(C) but
(D) or

( ) ❸ Let's leave now, otherwise we might _____.
(A) get caught in the rain
(B) stay a bit longer
(C) leave a little sooner
(D) not be late

Answer: C、D、A

❶ 句子意思是「你親自去看看吧，否則你永遠不會相信我說的話。」這裡需要選一個連接詞連接上下句。go and see for yourself 是祈使句，you will never believe me 是陳述句表結果，即如果第一句實現不了，就不會造成第二句的結果。根據這種逆意的條件關係，可斷定連接詞選 (C)。

❷ 句子意思是「把手舉起來，不然我就開槍了。」這應該是我們在警匪片中經常聽到員警對搶劫犯、強盜等危險分子說的話，四個選項都是連接詞，但根據逆意的條件關係，可判斷選 (D)。

❸ 句子的意思是：「我們現在走吧，不然我們可能會被雨淋濕的。」otherwise 之後的內容講述的是如果沒有「leave now」（現在離開）可能會造成的後果，其中 (C)「提早離開」、(D)「不遲到」都不是現在沒有離開會造成的後果，而 (B)「待久一點」雖然確實是現在沒有離開會造成的後果，但現在沒有離開的話，本來就一定會待久一點，所以句中的 might（可能）就變成多餘的了。因此只有 (A) 為正確答案。

more than...

我們常說「他不只是朋友而已」或「我得這個病已經超過十年了」，其中的「不只……」或「超過……」都可以用這個句型來表示。

 關鍵句型 **點**

❶ 根據more than後面接的語詞不同，又分為以下幾個句型搭配：
  ・句型「more than＋數詞」，表示「……以上、不止……」之意。此時，相當於over，兩者可以互換。
  例 I have known him for **more than** 20 years.
    →我已經認識他超過 20 年了。

  ・句型「more than ＋名詞」，表示「不只是；不僅僅是」。
  例 He is **more than** a famous artist; he is a director, too.
    →他不僅僅是個著名的畫家，還是個導演。

  ・句型「more than ＋形容詞 / 副詞」表示「很；非常；尤其」的意思。此時，與 very 同義。
  例 I am **more than** satisfied with the job.
    →我非常滿意這份工作。

❷ 另外，與「more than＋形容詞/副詞」相反的句型是「less than＋形容詞/副詞」，意為「不，很少，不很，不到」，具有否定意義。

會話演練 **線**

會話翻譯

A Are you sure he's telling the truth?

B Yes, I'm sure, for I have known him for **more than** 20 years.

A: 你確信他是誠實的嗎？

B: 是的，我確信，因為我已經認識他超過 20 年了。

A How are you getting on with your new job?

B Quite well. I am **more than** satisfied with the job.

A: 你的新工作進展得怎麼樣了？

B: 很好。我非常滿意這份工作。

A How do you like my hometown?

B The beauty is **more than** I can describe.

A: 你覺得我的家鄉怎麼樣？

B: 美得無法形容。

A Is he an artist?

B He is **more than** a famous artist; he is a director, too.

A: 他是個畫家嗎？

B: 當然。他不僅僅是個著名的畫家，還是個導演。

例句 一連發

1 Altogether **more than** 70 percent of the surface of our planet is covered by water.
整體說來，我們這個星球表面有 70% 以上都被水所覆蓋。

2 Hibernation is **more than** sleep.
冬眠不僅僅是睡眠。

3 Modern science is **more than** a large amount of information.
現代科學不僅僅是大量的資訊。

4 Jason is **more than** a lecturer; he is a writer, too.
傑森不只是一個演說家，他也是一個作家。

5 This secret is **more than** we can afford to let out.
這個秘密我們是不能洩露的。

6 The doctor is **more than** careful in operations.
這個醫生動手術時非常細心。

7 He was **more than** pleased with her performance.
他對她的表演非常滿意。

8 I assure you she is **more than** glad to see you.
我敢保證她會非常高興見到你。

9 In class, he listens **more than** attentively.
在課堂上，他聽講十分專心。

10 We were busy and **less than** delighted to have visitors that day.
那天我們很忙，不高興有客人來。

小小試身手

( ) **❶** We advertised for pupils last autumn, and got _____
60.
(A) more than   (B) more of
(C) as much as   (D) so many as

( ) **❷** In doing scientific experiments, you must be _____
careful with the instruments.
(A) less than   (B) more than
(C) no more than   (D) no less than

( ) **❸** –I was _____ to see him.
–Why? Did you have a fight?
(A) more than happy   (B) less than happy
(C) more happier   (D) less happier

Answer: **A、B、B**

❶ 句子意思是「我們去年秋天登招生廣告，招到六十個以上的學生。」as much as 用於修飾不可數名詞，不能用來指學生人數。so...as... 一般用於否定句中。只有「more than ＋數詞」，表示「……以上、超過……、不止……」之意，相當於 over。所以答案選 (A)。

❷ 句子意思是「在做科學實驗時，你必須非常小心地使用儀器。」句型「more than ＋形容詞」在這裡的用法，相當於 very，表示「很、非常、尤其」的意思。「less than ＋形容詞」與「more than ＋形容詞」相反，意為「不、不很、不到」。no more than 意思是「至多，僅僅」；no less than 意思是「多達，不低於」。根據句子意思，more than careful 相當於 very careful，所以答案選 (B)。

❸ 句子的意思是：「我不是很開心看到他。」「為什麼？你們吵架了嗎？」由後句詢問吵架的事，可知前句說話者應該看到「him」時應該不是 happy 的感覺，不可使用 more than happy 的句型，只有 (B) less than happy 為正確答案。

比較級＋ than...

我們在比較兩個東西時，會說「這件衣服比我
上次買的那件還貴」或「我的年紀比她大多了」，
這時就可以用這個句型。

 關鍵句型 **點**

❶ 句型「比較級＋than」用於兩者的比較，意思是「A 比 B
更……」。在將兩者進行比較時，如果形容詞或副詞是單音節，
其比較級在詞尾加 -er，如果形容詞或副詞是多音節，其比較級
即在字首加 more。此外，必須用形容詞或副詞的比較級與 than
配合使用。為了避免重複，一般情況下可以把子句中與主句相
同的成分省略。

例 My bicycle is **cheaper than** yours(＝ your bicycle).
→我的腳踏車比你的（腳踏車）便宜。

❷ 在形容詞比較級前，還可以用much, a lot, a little, by far等來修
飾，表示程度。

例 But her sister is **much more beautiful than** her.
→但是她妹妹比她漂亮的多。

❸ 形容詞或副詞的比較級前有諸如no, not, never之類的否定詞時，
則該句型變為另一個句型：「否定詞＋比較級」。這個否定形式
的比較級句型表示的是肯定含義，意為「最、極」，有時候可以
表示最高級的含義。意為「再沒有比……更……的了」。

例 Nothing is **more valuable than** money.
→金錢比任何東西都珍貴。

會話演練

比較級＋than...

會話翻譯

A My bicycle is **cheaper than** yours.	A: 我的腳踏車比你的（腳踏車）便宜。
B But my bicycle is **lighter than** yours.	B: 但是我的腳踏車比你的（腳踏車）輕。

A Do you think she is beautiful?	A: 你認為她漂亮嗎？
B Yes. But her sister is **much more beautiful than** her.	B: 是的，她很漂亮。但是她妹妹比她漂亮的多。

A Nothing is **more valuable than** money.	A: 金錢比任何東西都珍貴。
B I don't think so.	B: 我不這樣認為。

A His shoes are **bigger than** mine.	A: 他的鞋子比我的還大。
B That's because his feet are **bigger than** yours.	B: 那是因為他的腳比你的還大。

❶ Facts speak **louder than** words.
事實勝於雄辯。

❷ Too much help is sometimes **worse than** no help.
太多的幫助有時候比沒有幫助更糟糕。

❸ Today is **much hotter than** yesterday.
今天比昨天熱多了。

❹ I am two years **older than** my brother.
我比我的弟弟大兩歲。

❺ The new boss is **by far better than** the last one.
這個新老闆比上一個老闆好多了。

❻ Nothing is **more important than** knowledge.
知識是最重要的。

❼ There is **no** idea **better than** this.
這個辦法再好不過了。

❽ I **couldn't** feel any **better**.
我感覺好極了。

❾ Nobody is **more selfish than** her in the class.
她是班上最自私的人了。

小小試身手

( ) ❶ The air in Taipei is getting much ____ now than a few years ago.
(A) clean   (B) cleaner
(C) cleanest   (D) the cleanest

( ) ❷ Now Helen works ____ than before.
(A) more carefully (B) more careful
(C) much careful   (D) much carefully

( ) ❸ Bob ran 100 meters in 9.91 seconds. I have not seen ____ this year.
(A) the best   (B) better
(C) the most   (D) more

Answer: **B、A、B**

❶ 句子的意思是「台北現在的空氣比幾年前的乾淨多了。」根據題目中的 than 可判斷這個句型是「比較級＋than」。將台北空氣的現在和幾年前作比較，所以要用形容詞的比較級形式，正確答案選 (B)。

❷ 句子的意思是「海倫現在比以前更謹慎工作了。」本題的關鍵在於副詞 carefully 的比較級形式。因為 carefully 是多音節單字，所以其比較級形式是在其前面加 more，正確答案是 (A)。

❸ 句子的意思是「鮑伯的 100 公尺跑了 9.91 秒，今年我沒有看到比這更好的成績了。」根據句中的否定字 not，可推斷是「否定詞＋比較級」句型，再根據題意可以判斷說話者要用否定形式的比較級表達肯定含義，意思是「再沒有比⋯⋯更⋯⋯的了」，所以答案選 (B)。

I'm afraid (that)...

「我擔心他不會答應。」或「恐怕生米已經煮成熟飯。」……等表示擔憂的語氣，都可以用這個句型來表達。

 關鍵句型 **點**

❶ I'm afraid that...在口語中使用非常廣泛，可以翻譯成「恐怕」。基本用法是：當說話者猜想自己告知對方的消息、情況等有可能造成對方不快、失望、煩惱或為難時，可以用I'm afraid that...來緩和語氣；或者當說話者單純出於措辭禮貌時，也可以用這個句型。相當於I'm sorry, but...。

例 **I'm afraid that** he's not available at the moment.
→抱歉，恐怕他現在可能沒有空。

❷ I'm afraid可以位於句首，後面接that子句。that常可以省略。

例 **I'm afraid** you are in my seat. →恐怕你坐到的是我的座位。

會話演練 **線**

會話翻譯

A What are you looking for?

B My Student ID. Ah, **I'm afraid** I left it in the dorm.

A: 你在找什麼呢？

B: 我的學生證，啊，我恐怕是把它放在宿舍了。

A Can I speak to Mr. Chang?

B **I'm afraid that** he's not available at the moment.

A: 我可以和張先生通話嗎？

B: 抱歉，恐怕他現在不能接電話。

A Excuse me; **I'm afraid** you are in my seat.

B Oh, dear.

A: 對不起，恐怕你坐的是我的座位。

B: 哎呀。

A **I'm afraid** I can't help you. I'm new here too.

B I'll ask someone else. Thanks anyway!

A: 恐怕我沒辦法幫你，我也是新來的。

B: 那我問別人好了。還是謝啦！

例句 一連發

❶ I'm afraid you are late.
恐怕你遲到了。

❷ I'm afraid he's out at the moment.
恐怕他此刻不在。

❸ I'm afraid (that) I can't help you.
我恐怕幫不了你。

❹ I'm afraid I'll have to cancel the appointment with you.
恐怕我不得不取消與你的預約。

❺ I'm afraid you don't see my point.
恐怕你沒弄懂我的意思。

❻ I'm afraid I've taken too much of your time.
我怕我佔用了你太多時間。

❼ I'm afraid that you still don't know the truth.
恐怕你還不了解真相吧！

❽ I'm afraid we can't finish it on time.
恐怕我們無法準時完成了。

( )❶ –I'd like to make an appointment with Doctor Liu this week.
–Well, let's see. _____ he is fully booked on Monday and Tuesday.
(A) I think   (B) I guess
(C) He said   (D) I'm afraid

( )❷ –My dear, why don't we buy a car?
–_____ we do not have enough money to buy a new car.
(A) I'm afraid   (B) I'll be afraid
(C) we are afraid   (D) we'll be afraid

Answer: **D、A**

❶ 句子意思是「我想本週預約劉醫師看病。」「嗯,我來看看。恐怕劉醫師本週星期一和星期二的預約都已經滿了。」這是一個醫院裡病人來掛號看病時常見的會話場景。因為掛號人員知道自己告知病人的消息會讓病人有所失望,為了讓病人感覺上舒坦一些,便可以用 I'm afraid that 的句型。that 常省略。故選 (D)。

❷ 句子的意思是「親愛的,我們為什麼不買一輛車呢?」「 我怕我們沒有足夠的錢買一輛新車。」這裡是用 I'm afraid that 的句型。老公為了在拒絕老婆的時候讓她感覺舒坦一些,就用了這個句型。但是需要特別注意的是,這個句型的人稱只能是 I,時態也只能用現在式,表示說話人說話當時的語氣和態度。所以只能選 (A)。

Unit 06 It is obvious/clear that...

我們常說的「顯然他並不瞭解你」或「很明顯地，他說的是假話」，這些句子都表示真相昭然若揭，都可以用這個句型來表達。

關鍵句型 點

❶ It is obvious/clear that...的意思是「清楚、顯然」。此句型借助先行詞it作為形式上的主詞，而把主詞即that引導的子句放在句尾。that可以省略。

 It is obvious that the driver couldn't control his car.
→那個司機明顯控制不住他的車了。

It is obvious that she won't see you.
→很顯然地，她並不想見你。

❷ 形容詞obvious和clear前面還可加副詞very, quite等來修飾。

 It is quite clear that it has been stolen.
→非常明顯，它被偷了。

會話演練 線

It is obvious/clear that...

會話翻譯

A **It is obvious that** the driver couldn't control his car.

B He must be drunk.

A: 那個司機明顯控制不住他的車了。

B: 他一定喝醉了。

A What a mess! Oh, my God! Where is my new computer?

B **It is** quite **clear that** it has been stolen.

A: 好亂啊！天哪！我的新電腦到哪裡去了？

B: 很明顯，它被偷了。

A Could you tell me how can I find Amanda?

B **It's obvious that** she won't see you.

A: 你能告訴我怎樣才能找到亞曼達嗎？

B: 很顯然地，她並不想見你。

A Is that your girlfriend?

B What? **Isn't it obvious that** she's my mom?

A: 那是你女朋友嗎？

B: 啊？她不是很明顯是我媽嗎？

例句**一連發**

① **It is obvious/clear that** she is terribly nervous on stage.
很明顯她在台上非常緊張。

② **It's clear that** you are wrong.
你顯然是錯的。

③ **It is clear that** she is the best student in the class.
很明顯，她是班上最好的學生。

④ **It is obvious that** he's suffered a great deal.
很顯然，他承受了巨大的痛苦。

⑤ **It is clear that** she will pass the exam.
顯而易見地，她會通過這次考試。

⑥ **It is quite clear that** the whole project is doomed to failure.
很清楚地，這整個計畫註定要失敗。

⑦ **It is very obvious that** he doesn't like you at all.
很顯然地，他一點也不喜歡你。

⑧ **It's clear that** I won't trust you any more.
我顯然不會再相信你了。

小小 試身手

( ) ❶ It is clear _____ you _____ Anna for his sister.
　　(A) X / mistook　　　　　　(B) X / should mistake
　　(C) that / mistaken　　　　(D) that / should mistake

( ) ❷ It is _____ that Bob _____ the composition himself.
　　(A) quite obvious / doesn't write
　　(B) quite obvious / didn't write
　　(C) obvious quite / didn't write
　　(D) obvious / doesn't write

( ) ❸ –Ben is such a great basketball player.
　　–Are you serious? _____ he barely knows the rules.
　　(A) It is an obvious　　　　(B) It is clearly
　　(C) Obvious　　　　　　　(D) It is obvious

Answer: **A、B、D**

❶ 句子意思是「很顯然，你誤把安娜當作是她妹妹。」這裡用的是句型 It is clear that...。it 作為形式上的主詞，而把主詞即 that 引導的子句放在句末。that 也可以省略。而 mistake...for... 是固定用法，意思是「把……誤當作……」，根據句子意思，子句要用一般過去式，而 mistaken 是 mistake 的過去分詞，不適用於此，所以選 (A)。

❷ 句子的意思是「很顯然，鮑伯不是自己寫這篇作文。」obvious 可以用程度副詞 quite 修飾，quite 要放在 obvious 前面，根據句意可知，子句陳述的事情已經過去，所以子句的動詞要用過去式，答案選 (B)。

❸ 句子的意思是：「班的籃球打得真好。」「你在開玩笑吧？很明顯他根本不懂規則。」此處唯一符合文法的就是 (D)，為正確答案。若要使用 clearly，前面就不需要加上 It is；而如果要用 it is，正確說法應為 It is clear。

It is a pity (shame/ surprise...) that...

我們常表現的情緒如「真可惜……」、「真遺憾……」、「真丟臉……」、「真令人驚訝……」等，都可以用這個句型來表達。

關鍵句型 點

❶ 句型「It is a pity (a shame/a surprise...) that ... 」表達的是說話者某種感情或感受，比如：驚奇、懊悔、失望、不滿等。子句的情況發生在主句情況之前。that後的子句一般用虛擬語氣，即：should＋原形動詞。should通常不能省略，用於加強說話人的語氣，有「居然、竟然」的意味。該句型子句中的動詞有兩種形式：should do或should have done。should do表示現在或將來發生的事，should have done表示過去發生的事情。

 It is a pity that our team **should** lose the game.
→我們隊伍輸掉了比賽，真是可惜。

❷ 如果該句型不表示驚奇等情感，that子句也可以用陳述語氣。

 It's a shame that she can't understand English.
→她聽不懂英文，真是遺憾。

會話演練 **線**

會話翻譯

It is a pity (shame/surprise...) that...

A **It is a pity that** our team **should** lose the game.

B We should train harder.

A: 我們隊伍輸掉了比賽，真是可惜。

B: 我們應該更嚴格地訓練。

A **It is a shame that** you **should** live at such a distance.

B Don't worry. I can always drive.

A: 你住得居然這麼遠，真是遺憾。

B: 別擔心，反正我可以開車。

A **It's a shame that** she can't understand English.

B Why not draw a map of the block for her?

A: 她聽不懂英文，真是遺憾。

B: 你為什麼不畫一張這個街區的地圖給她呢？

A **It's a pity that** you can't make it to the party.

B Yeah. Have fun without me!

A: 真可惜你沒辦法去參加派對。

B: 是啊，沒有我在，你們好好玩吧！

例句 一連發

❶ It is a shame that he **should** have failed the exam.
他竟沒通過考試，太可惜了！

❷ It is a shame that I wasted so much time.
我浪費了這麼多時間，真是慚愧。

❸ It's a pity that she **should** miss so important a lesson.
真遺憾，這麼重要的課她竟然錯過了。

❹ It is a pity that such a thing **should** happen in your class.
這種事竟然發生在你們班上，真是遺憾！

❺ It is a great pity that he **should** be so conceited.
真遺憾他竟會這樣自大。

❻ It is a shame that you **should** have to submit to his caprices.
你竟然受他的反覆無常所支配，真可恥。

❼ It is a pity that he is ill.
他生病了，真遺憾！

❽ It is a pity that he did not turn up at the meeting.
他沒有出席這次會議，真是遺憾。

( ) ❶ He didn't come back until the film ended. It was a pity that he _____ this film.
(A) missed (B) should miss
(C) have missed (D) should have missed

( ) ❷ It is a great pity that you _____ so careless.
(A) was (B) will be
(C) should be (D) be

( ) ❸ It's a pity that _____ miss such an important event.
(A) you (B) you have
(C) you should (D) you will be

Answer: **D、C、C**

❶ 句子的意思是「他直到電影結束才回來。他沒有看到這部電影真可惜。」根據句子意思可以看出，說話者表達出懊悔、失望之情。四個選項中只有 (B)、(D) 可以表達這種感情，其中的 should 有「居然、竟然」的意味。因為本題描述的是過去發生的事情，所以子句的動詞用「should have ＋過去分詞」。正確答案選 (D)。

❷ 句子的意思是「你這麼粗心，真是遺憾。」根據題意，本題想要表達的不在敘述現在事實本身，而在表達說話者失望、遺憾的感情，所以 that 後的子句用虛擬語氣：should ＋原形動詞。正確答案是 (C)。

❸ 句子的意思是：「真可惜你得錯過這麼重要的活動。」此處使用的是 It's a pity that sb. should... 的句型，表達發生句子後半所說的事很可惜之意，(C) 為正確答案。

How (What/When...) + to do...?

「我不知道該選哪一個」或「請告訴我接下來該怎麼做」，這些句子中都表達了疑惑，但並不是直接提出問題，而且間接地指出問題，這時便適合用這個句型。

 關鍵句型 **點**

❶ 這個句型是「特殊疑問詞＋不定詞」。其中的特殊疑問詞包括疑問代名詞who, whom, what, which, whose和疑問副詞when, where, how。此外，連接詞「whether」也適用。但是在英文中，沒有why to do it這個說法。

例 I don't know **which to choose**.
→我不知道該選哪一個。

❷ 「特殊疑問詞＋不定詞」這種結構常用在動詞tell, show, know, forget, find out, learn, teach, wonder, remember等單字後面，相當於名詞子句。

例 I don't know **what to say** next.
→我不知道接下來要說什麼。

會話翻譯

A I don't know **what to say** next.

B Take it easy. Outline what you want to say first.

A: 我不知道接下來要說什麼。

B: 放輕鬆，先列出你想要說的話。

A I don't know **which to choose**.

B Just go with the cheapest one.

A: 我不知道該選哪一個。

B: 那就選最便宜的吧。

A Why don't we drive to the amusement park?

B The problem is **where to park** the car.

A: 為什麼不開車去遊樂園？

B: 問題是要把車停在哪裡。

A We are not certain **whether to** get married or not.

B Why? Don't you love each other?

A: 我們還沒決定是否要結婚？

B: 為什麼？你們難道不相愛嗎？

❶ Where to make a turn is a difficult problem.
在哪裡轉彎是一個難題。

❷ I'll show you **how to operate** this machine.
我會示範如何操作這台機器。

❸ Lily has no idea **which room to clean** first.
莉莉不知道要先打掃哪間房間。

❹ The important thing is **where to find** the financial aid.
重要的事是去哪裡找到經濟援助。

❺ Doctor Chang told him **when to take** the medicine.
= Doctor Chang told him **when he should take** the medicine.
張醫生告訴他在什麼時候吃藥。

❻ I don't know **how to** quit smoking.
我不知道如何戒煙。

❼ What to do?
怎麼辦？

❽ How beautiful these skirts are! I can't make up my mind **which to buy.**
這些裙子多漂亮啊！我沒辦法決定要買哪一條。

❾ When to hold the meeting has not yet been decided.
還沒有決定什麼時候開會。

小小**試身手**

( ) ❶ The little girl cannot tell ____ to trust ____.
    (A) which / her   (B) whom / X
    (C) whom / her   (D) when / X

( ) ❷ When and where to go for this summer vacation
    _____ yet.
    (A) are not decided
    (B) have not been decided
    (C) is not being decided
    (D) has not been decided

( ) ❸ Do you know _____ the air conditioner on?
    (A) how turn   (B) how turning
    (C) how to turn   (D) how can turn

Answer: **B、D、C**

❶ 句子的意思是「小女孩不能辨別該相信誰。」在「特殊疑問詞＋不定詞」的句型中，首先要分析題目的句子。第一個空格填的疑問詞與後面的不定詞 to trust 合起來是當作 tell 的受詞。而 to trust 缺少自己的受詞，它前面的特殊疑問詞就應該是它的受詞，即「誰」。所以第二個空格什麼也不用填。答案為 (B)。

❷ 句子意思是「這個暑假去哪以及什麼時候去都還沒決定。」When and where to go for this summer vacation 是兩個疑問詞，但「兩個疑問詞＋不定詞」做主詞時，仍屬於「一個疑問詞＋不定詞」的句型，動詞仍要用單數形式，所以答案為 (D)。

❸ 句子的意思是：「你知道怎麼開冷氣嗎？」此處用的是 Do you know how to + 原 V 的句型，只有 (C) 是符合文法的正確答案。

Unit 09 There is no ＋名詞 ＋ (in) ＋ doing ...

「這樣做是沒有意義的。」或「再說下去也是沒有用的。」，這些句子中都強調「做某事是沒有……的。」都適合用這個句型。

關鍵句型 點

❶ 這是個There be引導的句型。句型的主詞是名詞後面的動名詞 doing。其中的介系詞in可以省略。用於這種句型的常見名詞 有：use, good, harm, sense, point等。不同名詞放在這個句型 中，意思也不盡相同：

 There is no use in trying to explain it. →解釋是沒有用的。

 There is no good in making friends with him.
　　→和他交朋友沒有什麼好處。

 Come on, **there is no harm** smoking one or two cigarettes a day. →拜託！一天抽一兩根煙沒有害處的。

 There is no point in arguing with him further.
　　→繼續和他爭論是沒有意義的。

❷ 同時，句型「There is＋no＋名詞＋(in)＋doing...」可以與句型 「It is＋no＋名詞＋doing...」互換。在it引導的這個句型中，it 作虛主詞，真正的主詞也是後置的動名詞doing。

會話演練 **線**

 會話演練 **線**

There is no ＋名詞＋ (in) ＋ doing ...

會話翻譯

A He is so stubborn that I couldn't persuade him.

B **There is no point in** arguing with him further.

A: 他太固執了，我說服不了他。

B: 繼續和他爭論是沒有意義的。

A You should give up smoking.

B Come on, **there is no harm** smoking one or two cigarettes a day.

A: 你應該戒煙。

B: 得了吧！一天抽一兩根煙沒有害處的。

A **There is no good in** making friends with him.

B I should have taken your advice earlier.

A: 和他交朋友沒有什麼好處。

B: 我應該早點聽你的忠告的。

A Please listen to me.

B **There is no use in** trying to explain.

A: 請聽我説。

B: 解釋是沒有用的。

例句**一連發**

❶ **There is no point in** joking about such matters.
拿這種事開玩笑是沒有意義的。

❷ **There is no point** in going out to date someone.
和別人出去約會是沒有意義的。

❸ **There is no use** talking to her again.
= **It's no use** talking to her again.
再跟她談也是沒有用的。

❹ **It is no use** crying over spilt milk.
覆水難收。

❺ **There is no sense** electing him chairman.
選他當主席是沒有道理的。

❻ **It's no good** (your) refusing to do it .
= **There is no good** (your) refusing to do it.
你拒絕做這件事是沒有好處的。

❼ **There is no sense (in)** making your mother angry.
惹你媽媽生氣是沒有意義的。

❽ **There is no point in** doing such stupid things.
做這種蠢事是沒有意義的。

小小試身手

Level

4

There is no ＋ 名詞 ＋ (in) ＋ doing …

(　) **❶** There is no point _____ for him.
(A) to wait
(B) that we wait
(C) on waiting
(D) in waiting

(　) **❷** There is no _____ trying to explain to me!
(A) use
(B) useful
(C) useless
(D) X

(　) **❸** Don't be so strict! There is no _____ in letting the kids play outside.
(A) point
(B) harm
(C) use
(D) good

Answer: **D、A、B**

❶ 句子意思是「沒有必要等他。」There is no point in doing sth. 這個句型的主詞是名詞後面的動名詞片語：waiting for him。尤其需要注意的是，這個動名詞片語不能換成不定詞，即不能錯寫為：There is no point to wait for him. 這個句型中的介系詞 in 可以省略，所以答案選 (D)。

❷ 句子意思是「再試圖向我解釋也沒有用。」句型 There is no ＋ 名詞 ＋ (in) doing sth. 的主詞是名詞後面的動名詞片語 trying to explain to me。這種句型中的 no 後面要接名詞。而這四個選項中只有 (A) 選項的 use 是名詞。There is no use doing sth. 意思是「做……是沒有用的」，相當於 There is useless doing sth.。也就是說如果題目的句子中去掉 no，就可以選 (C) 選項的 useless 了。所以答案選 (A)。

❸ 句子的意思是：「別那麼嚴苛嘛！讓孩子們在外面玩，沒什麼壞處的。」前句似乎在勸說對方允許孩子去外面玩，表示說話者覺得孩子出去外面玩應該沒什麼「壞處」，因此選擇 (B) 為正確答案。若選擇其他選項，則變成說話者覺得孩子們出去玩沒什麼意義、沒什麼益處，就與前句的態度衝突了。

Unit 10 sb. ＋ must/can/could/may/ might/need/should/ought to ＋ have ＋過去分詞 ...

「他一定已經把這件事公諸於世了。」或「我們早應該聽他的話。」這些句子表達了對過去事件的推斷或感觸，都適合用這個句型。

 關鍵句型 **點**

❶「must＋have＋過去分詞」只用於肯定句中，表示對過去發生的事情進行肯定的推測，語氣比較堅定，意思是「過去一定……」。

例 She **must have gone** by bus. →她一定是坐公車去的。

❷「can/could＋have＋done」表示對過去事情的假設，意思是「本來能夠做某事（而沒有做）。」「can't/couldn't＋have＋過去分詞」表示「過去不可能做過，一定沒做過。」

例 That **can't have been** true. →那一定不是真的。

❸「may/might＋have＋過去分詞」表示對已發生的動作進行不肯定的推測，might語氣稍弱，表示「過去可能做過某事」。

例 You **might have left** it in the hotel room.
→你也許把它留在飯店房間裡了。

❹「need＋have＋過去分詞」表示「本來需要做某事（而沒有做）」。「其否定形式」則表示「本來不需要做某事（而做了）」。

例 We **need not have** set off so early.
→我們原本就不必那麼早出發的。

會話演練 **線**

會話翻譯

A Linda has gone to work, but her bicycle is still here.

B She **must have gone** by bus.

A: 琳達去上班了，但是她的腳踏車還在這裡。

B: 她一定是坐公車去的。

A I can't find my wallet.

B You **might have left** it in the hotel room.

A: 我找不到錢包。

B: 你也許把它留在飯店房間裡了。

A She was so sad that she couldn't sleep.

B You **should not have told** her the bad news.

A: 她難過得難以入睡。

B: 你本不應該告訴她這個壞消息的。

A I heard they got divorced last month.

B That **can't have been** true.

A: 我聽說他們上個月離婚了。

B: 那一定不是真的。

sb. + must/can/could/may/might/need/should/ought to + have + 過去分詞 ...

例句 **一連發**

1 It **must have rained** last night, for the road is all wet.
昨天晚上一定下雨了，因為道路都是濕的。

2 You **must have been** mad to tell him the truth.
你一定是瘋了才會告訴他真相。

3 My sister met him at the theater yesterday morning, so he **couldn't have been studying** at home.
我姊姊昨天上午在電影院遇見他，所以他一定沒有在家讀書。

4 You **might have read** about it in the newspapers.
你可能已經在報紙上看過這個消息了。

5 They **might not have known** it beforehand.
他們事先可能不知道這件事。

6 You **needn't have come** to visit the factory in person.
你不必親自來工廠視察。

7 You **could have been** more considerate.
你本來可以更周到的。

8 She **ought not to have thrown** the old clothes away.
她本來不應該扔掉那些舊衣服的。

9 He **could have passed** the exam, but he was too careless.
他本來能夠通過考試，但是他太粗心了。

小小 **試身手**

( ) ❶ You _____ to have done silly things to your friends.
    (A) had ought   (B) hadn't ought
    (C) ought not   (D) didn't ought

( ) ❷ –I stayed at a hotel while in New York.
    –Oh, did you? You _____ with Bob.
    (A) could have stayed   (B) could stay
    (C) would stay   (D) might stay

( ) ❸ If I had known earlier, I _____ you.
    (A) need to have helped
    (B) could have helped
    (C) ought to helped
    (D) must have helped

Answer: **C、A、B**

❶ 句子的意思是「你本不應該對你的朋友做那樣的蠢事。」這裡用的是句型「ought to have＋過去分詞」的否定形式「ought not to have＋過去分詞」，答案選 (C)。

❷ 句子的意思是「在紐約時我住在飯店。」「噢！真的嗎？你本來可以去和鮑伯住在一起的。」這裡是句型「could have＋過去分詞」的用法。根據 stayed 的時態，可知這裡談論的是過去發生的事情。所以第二個人是表示對過去發生事情的推測，應該用「情態動詞＋have＋done」的形式，根據句意，有這種功能的只有 (A)，所以應該選 (A)。

❸ 句子的意思是：「如果我早點知道，我就會幫你了。」(B) 為正確答案。(A) 意為「必須要幫助你」，不符合一般生活情境（不太會有「一定非得幫助別人不可」的情況，幫別人忙通常應該是自願的，被逼就不叫幫忙了），(C) 不符合文法，還缺了一個 have，而 (D) 意為「當時應該有幫助你」，但前半句已經提到之前不曉得對方需要幫助，既然不曉得，根本不可能去幫助他，所以 (D) 也不對。

Level 4

過關大挑戰

❶ Keep the machine in a dry place, _____ it will rust.
(A) or
(B) and
(C) but
(D) so

❷ Could you speak louder? I'm afraid _____ clearly.
(A) to hear you
(B) of hearing you
(C) I can hear
(D) I can't hear you

❸ The _____ the man, the _____ he will be.
(A) younger, experiencer
(B) younger, experienced
(C) older, experienced
(D) older, more experienced

❹ _____ was last night _____ she wore a beautiful evening dress at the party.
(A) That / when
(B) That / that
(C) It / when
(D) It / that

❺ _____ is quite clear_____ she doesn't want to tell the truth.
(A) It / why
(B) That / X
(C) It / X
(D) That / that

6 Could you tell me _____ the bus terminal?
(A) where to get
(B) where to get to
(C) how to get
(D) how to get to

7 Modern science is _____ a large amount of information.
(A) only
(B) X
(C) not
(D) more than

8 I wish I _____ to the moon in a spaceship one day.
(A) can fly
(B) could fly
(C) will fly
(D) flew

9 I wish I _____ as young as you.
(A) am
(B) were
(C) can be
(D) will be

10 There is _____ use just _____ about the plan.
(A) not / talking
(B) not / to talk
(C) no / talking
(D) no / to talk

11 – Someone called you just now, Tom.
– It _____ my wife. She told me she would call me at noon.
(A) might be
(B) can't have been
(C) must have been
(D) mustn't have been

超詳細解析

❶ 本題的句型是「祈使句＋or/otherwise＋陳述句」。它的意思是「……，否則……」。前面的祈使句是條件，意思是「把機器放在乾燥的地方」；而後面的陳述句是結果，意思是「否則會生銹。」，答案選(A)。

❷ 本題用的是I'm afraid that的句型。當要禮貌婉轉地向對方說明一些情況，而這些情況有可能造成對方不快、失望、煩惱或為難時，可以用I'm afraid that...來緩和語氣，意思是「恐怕……」。afraid後面要接that引導的子句，其中的that常省略。根據could you speak louder?可以判斷說話人聽不清楚對方所說的話，所以說話者才會接著說「對不起，恐怕我沒聽清楚你所說的。」所以答案是(D)。

❸ 本題用到的句型是「the＋比較級，the＋比較級」，表示「越……，就越……」的意思。前後兩個the都需要接形容詞或副詞的比較級。根據常識，人應該是越老經驗越豐富，其次，experienced是多音節單字，比較級是在其前面加more，所以選(D)。

❹ 這裡用的是強調句型It was...that...的用法。首先，確定強調句型的引導詞是it，而不能用that, this等代替。另外，在本題中，被強調的部分是last night，此時，連接詞不能用when，而只能用that來連接，所以選(D)。

❺ 本題是句型It is clear that...的用法，意思是「很顯然的……」。clear前面可以有very, quite等程度副詞來加以修飾。此句型句首要用先行詞it作形式主詞，而把主詞即that引導的名詞子句放在句尾。但that可以省略。所以選(C)。

⑥ 本題用的是「特殊疑問詞＋不定詞」句型。the bus terminal是要到達的目的地，所以要用「get to＋地點」。句子的意思是「你能告訴我怎麼去公車終點站嗎？」所以正確答案是(D)。

⑦ 透過分析可以判斷現代科學應該是建立在收集瞭解大量資訊的基礎上，但又「不僅僅是大量的資訊」。只有more than後面接名詞時譯作「不止是」、「不僅僅是」的意思，所以最恰當的選項應該是(D)。

⑧ wish引導子句表示不太可能實現的主觀願望，要用虛擬語氣。句子的意思是「我希望有一天我能乘太空船去月球。」這顯然是表達對將來的美好願望和憧憬，所以要用「wish＋主詞＋would/should/could/might＋原形動詞」，選(B)。

⑨ wish後面接that子句是使用虛擬語氣，表示某種不太可能實現的主觀願望，它們都與事實相反。that經常被省略。本句表達的是說話者現在的願望，要用「wish＋主詞＋過去式」，答案選(B)。

⑩ 句型There is no use doing sth.的意思是「做……是沒有用的。」常用於這個句型的名詞還有good, harm, sense, point等，答案是(C)。

⑪ 這裡用的是句型「must＋have＋過去分詞」，表示對過去發生的事情或狀態進行肯定的推測，語氣比較堅定，意思是「過去一定……」。根據she told me she would call me at noon可知第二個說話者對電話是他妻子打來的這個推測是很有把握的，所以選(C)。

過關測驗解答

01~06: (A)(D)(D)(D)(C)(D)   07~11: (D)(B)(B)(C)(C)

16 種時態的 4 種時間和 4 種方式

在中文裡，若要表示事件是在什麼時間發生，不需要改變動詞的形式，只要在句子中加上表示時間的副詞即可，例如「我昨天晚上買了一雙鞋」，「我今天下午買了一雙鞋」，「我明天要買一雙鞋」。不難發現，這幾個句子的動作和關鍵字都是「買鞋」，要表示不同時間買鞋只需要在句子中分別加上「昨天晚上」、「今天下午」、「明天」等。但是在英文中，不同時間發生的事件必須要用不同的動詞形式來表示，這些各種的動詞形式就叫作時態。

英文中的時態包括時（time）和式（form）兩方面。時表示事件發生的時間，分為現在、過去、未來和過去未來四種時間；式表示事件的表現方式，分為簡單、進行、完成和完成進行四種方式。不同的時和式相結合就構成了英文中的 16 種時態。它們分別是：現在簡單式、現在進行式、現在完成式、現在完成進行式、過去式、過去進行式、過去完成式、過去完成進行式、未來簡單式、未來進行式、未來完成式、未來完成進行式、過去未來簡單式、過去未來進行式、過去未來完成式、過去未來完成進行式。其中比較常用的時態有以下六個：現在簡單式、現在進行式、過去簡單式、未來式、現在完成式、過去完成式。下面我們就要來瞭解一下這些常用的時態！

英文句型和時態的關係非常密切。有些句型有固定的時態，有些句型可以有多種時態，但是不同時態運用於不同的場合中，有時候甚至意思也會有所不同。

1 現在簡單式

1. 現在簡單式的構成：

通常由原形動詞表示，但當主詞是第三人稱單數時，原形動詞的字尾需要加 -s 或 -es，be 動詞和 have 則有特殊的人稱變化。

例： · I/We/You/They know the man.
　　　 我 / 我們 / 你（們）/ 他們認識這個人。

　　 · He/She knows the man.
　　　 他 / 她認識這個人。

　　 · I am eighteen years old now.
　　　 我現在 18 歲。

　　 · You are really a honest boy.
　　　 你真是個誠實的孩子。

　　 · They/We/You are good friends.
　　　 他們 / 我們 / 你們是好朋友。

　　 · He/She is a doctor.
　　　 他 / 她是個醫生。

　　 · I/We/You/They have six classes today.
　　　 我 / 我們 / 你（們）/ 他們今天有六堂課。

　　 · It has a big nose.
　　　 牠有一個大鼻子。

　　 · He/She has breakfast at home every day.
　　　 他 / 她每天在家吃早餐。

2. 現在簡單式的基本用法：

★ 表示現在經常性或習慣性的動作。

★ 表示現在的特徵或狀態。

★ 表示客觀事實與真理。

★ 用於現場解說、實況報導、圖片、電影說明等場景中。

★ 表示預計或安排將來要發生的動作或事情。

只有少數動詞，如 come, go, leave, begin, start, arrive, be 等可以用一般現在式來表示計畫、安排將要發生的動作或事情。

2▶現在進行式

1. 現在進行式的構成：

由「主詞＋ am(is/are) ＋動詞的現在分詞」表示。

例：I am sending an e-mail to my parents.
我正在發電子郵件給我的父母。

He/She/It is sleeping.
他 / 她 / 牠正在睡覺。

You are sneezing.
你正在打噴嚏。

2. 現在進行式的基本用法：

★ 表示此時此刻正在發生或進行的動作。

★ 表示現階段正在發生或進行的動作。

★ 表示最近按計劃、安排將要發生的動作。

★ 表示反覆出現或習慣性的動作。這種用法含有不滿、厭煩、
遺憾等感情色彩，常與副詞 always, constantly 等連用。

3▶過去簡單式

1. 過去簡單式的構成：由動詞的過去式表示，動詞 be 則有
was 和 were 兩個過去式。

例：He took off his coat.
他脫掉了他的外套。

She/He was poor years ago.
幾年前她 / 他很窮。

We/You/They were there just now.
我們 / 你 (們)/ 他們剛才還在那裡。

2. 過去簡單式的基本用法：

★ 表示過去某時間發生的動作或存在狀態。

★ 表示過去經常或反覆發生的動作。

　　此時，常與表示頻率的時間副詞 often, always, usually 等連用。
如果這種過去經常反覆發生的動作現在已經中止，成為過去的習
慣，就要用 used to do sth.。

4▷ 未來簡單式

1. 未來簡單式的構成：一般由「shall/will ＋原形動詞」表示。

例：I/We shall go to Tokyo next week.
我 / 我們下週會去東京一趟。
I/We/They/He/She will be back in a few days.
我 / 我們 / 他們 / 他 / 她將在幾天後回來。
You will forget the sad news soon.
你很快就會忘記這件傷心事。

2. 未來簡單式的基本用法：

★ 表示將來某時間發生的動作或存在的狀態。

★ 表示說話人對將來的打算、意願、看法、猜測和設想等。

★ 表示將來某時間發生的動作或存在的狀態。

5▷ 現在完成式

1. 現在完成式的構成：一般由「have/has ＋動詞過去分詞」
表示

例：I/You/We/They have already worked for four hours.
我 / 你 (們)/ 我們 / 他們已經工作四個小時了。

He/She has visited the Louvre three times.
他 / 她已經參觀羅浮宮三次了。

2. 現在完成式的基本用法：

★ 表示過去發生現在已結束、但對現在造成影響的動作

例：在句型「It is the ＋序數＋ time ＋ that 子句」中的 that 子句就常用現在完成式。

★ 表示過去發生、且一直延續到現在的動作，常與「since ＋時間點」、「for ＋時間段」、these days、recently 等時間副詞連用。

6▷過去完成式

1. 過去完成式的構成：

一般由「had ＋動詞過去分詞」表示。

例：We had learned 1000 English words by the end of last term. 到上學期末為止，我們已經學會了 1000 個英文單字了。
　　He had fixed his car by the time we got there.
　　當我們抵達那裡時，他已經把車修好了。

2. 過去完成式的基本用法：

★ 表示事件在過去某一時間以前就已經發生並完成，或一直持續到這一過去時間。

此種情況通常與表示過去時間的副詞，如 by, for, since, until 等連用，或用於 before, when, until 等引導的時間副詞子句中，例如句型「by the time (that) ＋時間子句」。

Level 5

On the one hand, ... on the other hand...

我們常說的「一方面，他對陌生人很慷慨，另一方面，他對家人卻很吝嗇」，像這樣以不同角度來觀看事物的兩面時，便適合用這個句型。

 關鍵句型 **點**

❶ 這個句型指一個事情或事物的兩個方面，多用於引導出互相矛盾的兩個方面或觀點，意思是「一方面……，另一方面……」。在結構上，on the one hand和on the other hand引導的兩方面內容，要用逗號隔開。但是如果on the other hand置於句末時，前面就可以不用逗號。

例 **On one hand**, I really want to go, but **on the other hand**, I have to look after my sick baby. →一方面我非常想去，但另一方面，我必須照顧我生病的寶寶。

❷ 另外，on (the) one hand不可單獨使用，而須與on the other (hand) 並用，但on the other hand則可單獨使用。

例 The dresses here are beautiful and modern, but **on the other hand**, They are too expensive.
→這裡的洋裝漂亮又時髦，但是另一方面太貴了。

會話演練 線

A Could you come to my birthday party?

B **On one hand**, I really want to go, **but on the other hand**, I have to look after my sick baby.

A: 你能來參加我的生日派對嗎？

B: 一方面我非常想去，但另一方面，我必須照顧我生病的寶寶。

A What shall I do if I meet many strangers there?

B **On the one hand**, you shouldn't be shy; **on the other hand**, you mustn't forget your manners.

A: 如果我在那裡遇見好多陌生人該怎麼辦啊？

B: 一方面你不應該拘束，另一方面也不要放肆無禮。

A How do you like the dresses here?

B The dresses here are beautiful and modern, but **on the other hand**, they are too expensive.

A: 你認為這裡的洋裝怎麼樣？

B: 這裡的洋裝漂亮又時髦，但是另一方面太貴了。

A Should we go swimming tomorrow?

B **On one hand,** I'm a bit busy, **but on the other hand,** I do need some exercise.

A: 我們明天要不要去游泳？

B: 一方面我有點忙，但另一方面，我又確實需要運動了。

Level

5

On the one hand, ... on the other hand...

例句**一連發**

❶ On one hand, I am your teacher, and **on the other**, I am also your friend.
一方面我是你的老師,另一方面,我也是你的朋友。

❷ On one hand I want to settle down and get a job; **on the other hand** I want to go abroad for further study.
一方面我想安定下來,找個工作;另一方面我又想出國深造。

❸ What he said has been criticized **on one hand** and lauded **on the other hand**.
他說的話一方面受到批評,另一方面又受到稱讚。

❹ On one hand, we shouldn't always believe in them, but **on the other (hand)**, we should help them.
一方面,我們不能完全信任他們,但另一方面,我們應該幫助他們。

❺ On one hand I'm very happy because I can go home soon; **on the other hand**, I'm fairly worried because I have little money.
一方面就要回家了,我很高興;另一方面,我很擔心,我幾乎沒什麼錢了。

❻ The boy is clever, but **on the other hand**, he is too lazy.
這個男孩很聰明,但同時他又太懶惰了。

小小 **試身手**

( ) ❶ He has been criticized _____ and encouraged _____.
   (A) on one hand / on other hand
   (B) in one hand / in other hand
   (C) on the one hand / on the other
   (D) in one hand / in the other hand

( ) ❷ On one hand, she _____ his present; _____, she refused his invitation.
   (A) accepts / but
   (B) accepted / X
   (C) accepts / on other hand
   (D) accepted / but on the other hand

On the one hand, ... on the other hand...

Answer: **C、D**

❶ 句子的意思是「他一方面受到批評，另一方面卻受到鼓勵。」這裡要注意的是這個句型 on (the) one hand,...on the other (hand)。其中 on the one hand 的 the 可以被省略，on the other hand 的 hand 也可以被省略。另外，on the other hand 還可以放在句末，此時前面就可以不用逗號。所以答案選 (C)。

❷ 句子意思是「一方面她接受了他的禮物；但另一方面她又拒絕了他的邀請。」on (the) one hand,...on the other (hand) 這個句型可以用來說明事情互相矛盾的兩個方面，可以靈活翻譯成「一方面……，可是另一方面（同時）……。」從 refused his invitation 可以看出是過去式，根據上下語境判斷，前面也要用過去式 accepted。另外，on (the) one hand 不可單獨使用，而須與 on the other (hand) 並用。所以答案是 (D)。

both... and...

「我和他都是籃球隊的隊員。」或「她既聰明又美麗。」這些句子中都強調「兩者兼具」的特性，所以適合用這個句型。

 關鍵句型

❶ both... and...可說是一個並列連接詞，表示「……和……都」或「既……又……」。both... and...可以連接名詞、代名詞、動詞、形容詞、介系詞等，

例 We should tie up **both** his hands **and** his feet.
→我們應該把他的手腳都綁起來。

❷ 講到both... and...就不能不提到下面兩個相關句型：
- neither... nor...：表示對兩者否定，是both...and...的對立結構，意為「既不……也不……」。
- either... or...：表示兩者之間進行選擇，兩者之一，意為「……或者……」、「不是……就是……」。

例 The sweaters I tried were **either** too big **or** too small.
→我試穿的這幾件毛衣不是太大就是太小。

❸ 需要區分的一點是，當句型both... and...連接兩個名詞作主詞時，動詞通常用複數形式。而當句型either... or...和句型neither... nor...連接兩個主詞時，動詞在人稱和單複數都必須與它較近的主詞保持一致，也就是我們常說的「就近原則」。

例 **Both** Leah **and** Wayne are good at playing the violin.
→莉亞和維恩都擅長拉小提琴。

Neither these ones **nor** that one is a real gold ring.
→不管是這些還是那個，都不是真的金戒指。

會話演練 線

A We should tie up **both** his hands **and** his feet.

A: 我們應該把他的手腳都綁起來。

B Why don't we send him to the police station right away?

B: 為什麼不快點把他送到警察局去？

A How about these kinds of sweaters?

A: 這幾種毛衣怎麼樣？

B The sweaters I tried were **either** too big **or** too small.

B: 我試穿的這幾種不是太大就是太小。

A Who can play the violin, Leah or Wayne?

A: 莉亞和維恩誰會拉小提琴？

B **Both** Leah **and** Wayne are good at playing the violin.

B: 莉亞和維恩都擅長拉小提琴。

A I can't tell which gold ring is real.

A: 我辨別不出來哪個金戒指是真的。

B **Neither** these ones **nor** that one is a real gold ring.

B: 不管是這些還是那個都不是真的金戒指。

例句一連發

❶ Both Mr. Baker **and** his wife are very fond of music.
貝克先生和他的妻子都很喜歡音樂。

❷ **Both** John **and** Ann have got pen pals.
約翰和安都有筆友。

❸ We visited **both** New York **and** London.
我們不但訪問了紐約，還訪問了倫敦。

❹ A man should have **both** courage **and** wisdom.
人既要有勇氣，又要有智慧。

❺ The novel is popular **both** in Holland **and** in Denmark.
這本小說在荷蘭和丹麥都很流行。

❻ He can **neither** sing **nor** dance.
他既不會唱歌，也不會跳舞。

❼ **Neither** my dad **nor** my mom is at home today.
今天我父母都不在家。

❽ The show is **neither** exciting **nor** interesting.
那個表演既不刺激也不有趣。

❾ She **either** watches TV **or** reads novels at night.
晚上她不是看電視就是看小說。

❿ **Either** you **or** Tom is the champion.
冠軍不是你就是湯姆。

⓫ **Either** you **or** I am right.
要麼你對，要麼我對。

小小試身手

( ) **❶** The genius can ____ play the piano ____ compose music.
    (A) neither / nor   (B) either / or
    (C) both / and   (D) not / but

( ) **❷** Both rice and wheat ____ grown in that area.
    (A) is   (B) are
    (C) was   (D) were

( ) **❸** – ____ my brother ____ I can speak seven languages.
    –That's only normal. Not many can do that.
    (A) Not / only   (B) Neither / nor
    (C) Both / and   (D) Either / or

Level

5

both... and...

Answer: **C、B、B**

❶ 句子意思是「這個天才既會彈鋼琴又會作曲。」neither...
nor...表示對兩者否定，意為「既不……也不……」。either...
or...表示兩者之間進行選擇，意為「不是……就是……」。
both... and...表示「既……又……」，從句意可以判斷，既然是
genius，那麼這個人一定是play the piano和compose music兩
方面都擅長，所以選(C)。

❷ 句子意思是「那個地區既種植稻米又種植小麥。」rice和wheat
是兩種品種的作物，由both... and...連接，作為並列主詞，所以
動詞通常用複數形式。根據句意，這是指一般情況，所以用一
般現在式較適合，所以答案選(B)。

❸ 句子的意思是：「我哥哥和我都不會講七種語言。」「這很正
常的，本來就沒有多少人會講七種語言。」由答者所說的內容，
可以推測第一句的說話者所說的並不是哥哥與自己「都會」七
種語言，而應是「都不會」七種語言，所以只能選擇 (B) 為正
確答案。

我們常說的「我寧願死也不願給你半毛錢。」
或「我寧可在家睡覺也不想去參加那個無聊的晚
會。」都強調較喜歡 A 而較不喜歡 B，這種情形便
可以用這個句型來表達。

關鍵句型 **點**

❶ 這個句型的完整結構是：prefer to do sth. rather than do sth.。它主要用來表示選擇，意思是「比較喜歡……，而不喜歡……」、「寧願做……而不願做……」本句型中，prefer後面要加to不定詞，而rather than後面則接原形動詞。

 I **prefer to** take a train to Taipei **rather than** fly there.
→我寧願搭火車去台北，也不願意搭飛機去那裡。

❷ 還有幾個表示在兩者之間有所偏好或有所選擇的句型，例如：
- 「prefer ＋名詞 / 動名詞＋ to ＋名詞 / 動名詞」這個句型的意思是「寧願選……而捨棄……」，「比較喜歡……，而不喜歡……」。to 在這個句型中是介系詞而不是不定詞，後面必須接名詞或動名詞。

 I **prefer** jazz music **to** rock music.
→比起搖滾樂，我更喜歡爵士樂。

- would rather do... than do...意思是「寧願……而不願……」。would rather和than後面都接原形動詞。但是如果前後選用的動詞相同，那麼than後面的動詞常可以省略。

 I **would rather** stay at home **than** go there.
→我寧願待在家裡也不願去那裡。

會話演練 線

A How about going to Taipei by air?

B I **prefer to** take a train to Taipei **rather than** fly there.

A: 搭飛機去台北怎麼樣？

B: 我寧願搭火車去台北，也不願意搭飛機去那裡。

A Tell me why you are crying.

B I **prefer** to tell my doll **rather than** tell you.

A: 告訴我你為什麼哭。

B: 我寧願告訴我的洋娃娃也不想告訴你。

A Shall we drive to the countryside?

B I **would rather** stay at home **than** go there.

A: 我們開車去鄉下好嗎？

B: 我寧願待在家裡也不願去那裡。

A Do you like rock music?

B I **prefer** jazz music **to** rock music.

A: 你喜歡搖滾樂嗎？

B: 比起搖滾樂，我更喜歡爵士樂。

prefer to... rather than...

例句一連發

❶ I **prefer to** go to find out what on earth has happened **rather than** sit here waiting.
我寧願去搞清楚到底發生什麼事，也不願坐在這裡等待。

❷ We **prefer to** work extra hours this night **rather than** leave the work until the next week.
我們寧願今天晚上加班，也不願把工作留到下個星期。

❸ She **preferred** to go with us **rather than** stay with him.
她寧願和我們一起去，而不願和他待在一起。

❹ The students **prefer** to join in the game **rather than** watch it.
學生們喜歡參加比賽而不願只是觀看。

❺ He **prefers** doing **to** talking.
他喜歡做事，不喜歡說話。

❻ I **preferred** my old skirt **to** your new skirt.
我寧願穿我的舊裙子也不願穿你的新裙子。

❼ I'd rather take the slowest train **than** go there by air.
我寧願坐最慢的火車，也不搭飛機去那裡。

❽ I **would rather** have noodles **than (have)** rice.
我寧願吃麵也不吃飯。

小小試身手

( )❶ He always prefers _____ a bicycle rather than _____ on a crowded bus.
(A) ride / ride
(B) riding / ride
(C) to ride / ride
(D) riding / riding

( )❷ I would rather _____ in a quite place than _____ in a big restaurant.
(A) to eat / to eat
(B) eat / eat
(C) to eat / eating
(D) eating / eating

( )❸ I'd rather _____ than kiss a spider.
(A) dying
(B) dyeing
(C) die
(D) to dye

Answer: **C、B、C**

❶ 句子的意思是「他總是喜歡騎自行車，而不喜歡坐公車。」 prefer to do sth. rather than do sth. 這個句型表示兩者之間的挑選，意思是「比較喜歡……，而不喜歡……」，其中的 prefer 後面要接 to 不定詞，而 rather than 後面要接原形動詞。所以答案是 (C)。

❷ 句子的意思是「我寧願在一個安靜的地方吃飯也不願意在大餐廳裡吃飯。」 would rather do... than do... 的意思是「寧願……而不願」。 would rather 和 than 後面都要接原形動詞。所以正確答案是 (B)。

❸ 句子的意思是：「吻蜘蛛，毋寧死。」 would rather 之後需接原形動詞，只有 (C) 為正確答案。此外 dye 為「染色」的意思。

235

我們常說的「我之所以不告訴你真相是因為怕你難過。」或「她出國的理由是為了逃避她的家人。」這些句子當中都說明了兩件事情之間的因果關係，所以適合用這個句型。

 關鍵句型 **點**

❶ 這個句型表示「……的原因是……」的意思。這個句型結構比較複雜：句子的主詞是the reason，後面有兩個複合句。一個是關係副詞why所引導的子句，修飾句子的主詞the reason。一個是that所引導的子句。that不能省略。

例 **The reason why** she was fired **was that** the boss was not satisfied with her job.

→她被炒魷魚的原因是老闆對她的工作不滿意。

❷ 另外，這個句型還可以簡化為：The reason is/was that...。也就是把這個句型中why引導的子句去掉。

例 **The reason is that** I took a wrong bus.

→（我遲到的）原因是我坐錯公車了。

會話演練 **線**

會話翻譯

A You are late, Dennis.

B **The reason is that** I took a wrong bus.

A: 丹尼斯，你遲到了！

B: 我遲到的原因是我坐錯公車了。

A Could you tell me the truth, please?

B Well, **the reason why** he wants to leave you **is that** he is dying.

A: 請你告訴我真相，可以嗎？

B: 好吧。他想要離開你的原因是他快要死了。

A **The reason why** she was fired **was that** the boss was not satisfied with her job.

B To be frank, she is not fit for the job.

A: 她被炒魷魚的原因是老闆對她的工作不滿意。

B: 老實說，這個工作不適合她。

A **The reason** I can't attend the meeting **is that** I'll be overseas on a business trip.

B I see. I'll let my boss know.

A: 我沒辦法去開會的原因是我要到國外出差。

B: 瞭解了，我會告知我老闆的。

例句一連發

❶ **The reason why I** was sad **was that** you didn't understand me.
我難過的原因是你不瞭解我。

❷ **The reason why** he was late **was that** he missed the early bus.
他遲到的原因是他沒趕上早班車。

❸ **The reason why** I missed the train **was that** I got up late.
我沒趕上火車的原因是我睡過頭了。

❹ **The reason why** we have to grow trees **is that** they can provide us with fresh air.
我們必須種樹的原因是它們能供應我們新鮮的空氣。

❺ **The reason why** Susan is absent from school is that she is seriously ill.
蘇珊沒來上學的原因是她病得很重。

❻ **The reason why** he has achieved such success **is that** he never gives up.
他獲得如此成就的原因是他從不放棄。

❼ **The reason is that** we didn't finish the task on time.
原因是我們沒有按時完成任務。

小小試身手

( ) **❶** The reason _____ I can't come is that I have to prepare for the coming exam.
    (A) for   (B) as
    (C) because   (D) why

( ) **❷** The reason I did not go to France was _____ a new job.
    (A) that I got   (B) because of
    (C) due to   (D) because I got

( ) **❸** The reason he doesn't like mangoes _____ its smell makes him nauseous.
    (A) due to   (B) is because of
    (C) is that   (D) is due

Answer: **D、A、C**

❶ 句子的意思是「我不能來的原因是我必須準備馬上來臨的考試。」這裡是句型 The reason why... is that 的用法。reason 表示原因，why 引導的子句是修飾 the reason，答案為 (D)。

❷ 句子的意思是「我不去法國的原因是我找到了新工作。」當 reason 作主詞時，其後面的子句只能用 that 引導，而不能用連接詞 because 來引導，因此 (A) 選項為正確答案。

❸ 句子的意思是：「他不喜歡芒果的原因，是因為芒果的氣味讓他覺得噁心。」此句使用了 The reason... is that... 的句型，(C) 為正確答案。(A) 與 (B) 的後面必須接名詞片語，而 (D) 不符合文法。

even if/though...

「即使你出面，這件事也沒有轉圜的餘地」或「就算我幫你，你也不可能打敗他。」這些句子中都隱含著無奈的意味，便可以用這個句型。

 關鍵句型 **點**

❶ even if/even though...表示「即使……」、「縱使……」、「儘管……」。它們常可互換使用，但意義有細微差別。

❷ even if引導的子句強調子句含有較強的假設性，even though引導的子句則是以子句的內容為先決條件，也就是說，說話人肯定了子句的事實。

❸ even if/even though...引導的子句可以放在主句後也可以放在句首。

例 She won't leave the TV set **even if** there are no good programs on. →即使沒有好節目，她就是不離開電視機。
Even though he did say so, we cannot be sure he was telling the truth.
→即使他這麼說，我們也不能確信他的話是真的。

會話演練

會話翻譯

A Why is she always watching TV?

B She is a TV addict. She won't leave the TV set **even if** there are no good programs on.

A: 她為什麼總是在看電視？

B: 她是個電視迷。即使沒什麼好節目，她就是不離開電視機。

A He said he hadn't witnessed the accident.

B **Even though** he did say so, we cannot be sure he was telling the truth.

A: 他說他沒有親眼目擊這次意外事故。

B: 即使他這麼說，我們也不能確信他的話是真的。

A He is so rich!

B **Even if** he is a millionaire, he is unable to buy everything.

A: 他好有錢！

B: 即使他是個百萬富翁，他也無法買到所有的東西。

A **Even though** I apologized, he still wouldn't forgive me.

B Well, what did you expect? You crashed his new car!

A: 雖然我已經道歉了，他還是不肯原諒我。

B: 那不然你以為會怎樣？你可是撞壞了他的新車耶！

例句一連發

❶ I like to study English **even if/even though** it is rather difficult for me.

我喜歡學英文，儘管它對我來說相當難。

❷ We will back you up **even if/even though** you don't succeed.

儘管你不成功，我們也仍會支持你。

❸ **Even though** I didn't know anybody at the party, I had a good time.

儘管這次的派對上我誰也不認識，我還是玩得很開心。

❹ He is working in the office **even though** it is midnight.

儘管是午夜了，他還在辦公室裡工作。

❺ **Even though** he promises to keep the secret, we don't really trust him.

儘管他答應保守秘密，但我們並不真的信任他。

❻ Remember, science requires your whole life. And **even if** you had two lives to give, they would not be enough.

記住，科學需要你獻出一生，即使你有兩次生命可以奉獻也是不夠的。

小小試身手

( ) ❶ I will never forgive her _____ she says sorry to me.
    (A) as if   (B) after
    (C) even if   (D) if

( ) ❷ Even _____ you could fly as freely as the birds, you have to land on the earth one day.
    (A) if   (B) although
    (C) whether   (D) weather

( ) ❸ –Maybe your parents will agree to let you come to the party.
    –I won't be able to go _____ they agree. I'm super sick.
    (A) even though   (B) even if
    (C) even   (D) even had

Level 5

even if/though...

Answer: C、A、B

❶ 句子意思是「即使她向我說抱歉，我也永遠不會原諒她。」as if 是「好像」；after 是「在什麼之後」；if 是「如果……」，都不符合句子含義和邏輯關係，只有 even if「即使；儘管……」可以表達出這種讓步關係和句子含義，所以答案是 (C)。

❷ 句子意思是「即使你能夠像小鳥一樣自由飛翔，總有一天你還是得回到地面上來。」even if... 表示「即使；儘管……」。whether 表示「是否」；weather 表示「天氣」。這裡最容易搞混的就是 (B) 選項，although 也可以表示「儘管；雖然」，但它不能與 even 連用。所以正確答案是 (A)。

❸ 句子的意思是：「說不定你的父母會同意你來參加派對。」「就算他們答應也沒用，我病得超重的。」需注意 even though 與 even if 的差別。若此處選用 even though，句意會變成「雖然我父母答應我可以去參加派對，但我還是不能去」，父母是「已經答應了」的狀態。然而第二位說話者的父母並沒有「已經答應」，否則第一位說話者就不會說「說不定你父母會答應」，因此只能選擇表示「就算……」的 (B) 為正確答案。

Unit 06 have... do/doing/done...

在中文裡，我們說「我想讓你嚐嚐這個滋味」或「將行李打包」等，這些句子中的「你」和「行李」都是處於被動地位，在英文裡便是用這個句型來表達。

 關鍵句型 點

這個句型是由使役動詞have後接原形動詞、現在分詞或過去分詞所構成的複合結構。大致分為以下幾種意涵：

❶ have sb. V：這個句型結構意為「讓／請某人做某事」，這個動作是一次性的具體動作，且在當時尚未發生。

例 I will be glad to **have** you **read** it to us.
→我很高興由你讀這個給我們聽。

❷ have sb./sth. V-ing：這個句型結構表示「使某人／物一直處於某種狀態」，後面常接一段時間。此時have也可由keep來代替。

例 She **had** the poor baby **crying** for about 30 minutes.
→她任憑這個可憐的嬰兒哭了大約半小時。

❸ have sb.sth. V-ed：這個結構一般有以下兩種不同的意思：

・表示「讓某人被....讓某事被....」，強調這不是主詞親自做的，而是由別人做的。

例 I'd like to **have** this package **weighed**.
→我想秤一下這個包裹的重量。

・表示「遭受到某種事情」，說明遭遇的是無法控制的意外事故、自然災害等，並不著重說明「是誰使他遭遇這種災難。」

例 I **had** my phone **stolen**. →我的手機被偷了。

會話演練 線

會話翻譯

A Good morning. Can I help you?

B I'd like to **have** this package **weighed**.

A: 早安！我能幫你嗎？

B: 我想秤一下這個包裹的重量。

A May I read the poem for everyone?

B Certainly. I will be glad to **have** you **read** it to us.

A: 我可以為大家讀這首詩嗎？

B: 當然可以。我很高興由你讀這首詩給我們聽。

A She **had** the poor baby **crying** for about 30 minutes.

B She is too young to take care of the baby.

A: 她任憑這個可憐的嬰兒哭了大約半小時。

B: 她太年輕，不會照顧嬰兒。

A I **had** my cell phone **stolen** on my way home this afternoon.

B What rotten luck!

A: 今天下午我在回家的路上，手機被偷了。

B: 運氣真背！

245

例句**一連發**

1 We **had** Alice **attend** that meeting with him.
我們讓愛麗絲與他一起參加那個會議。

2 **Have** the next patient **come** in now please.
現在請讓下一位病人進來。

3 I won't **have** him **cheat** me any more.
我不會再讓他騙我了。

4 His parents **had** him **staying** at home all the time.
他父母親讓他一直待在家裡。

5 We **have** never **had** women **working** in this department of our company before.
我們以前從來沒有讓女性在公司的這個部門工作過。

6 Don't shout! You'll **have** the neighbors **complaining**.
別叫了！你會讓鄰居們抗議的。

7 He wants to **have** his microwave **repaired**.
他想請人修理他的微波爐。

8 Mrs. Smith **had** two of her teeth **taken** out last week.
上個星期史密斯夫人請人拔掉她的兩顆牙齒。

9 Houses near airports sometimes have their windows **broken**.
機場附近的房子的玻璃有時候會被震裂。

10 They **had** their request **refused**.
他們的請求遭到拒絕。

小小 試身手

( ) ❶ The night before the procession, the two cheaters ____ their lights ____ all night long.
(A) have / burning   (B) had / burning
(C) had / burned   (D) had / burn

( ) ❷ This morning I had my finger ____.
(A) cutting   (B) to cut
(C) to be cutting   (D) cut

( ) ❸ I had my brother ____ the garbage out for me.
(A) take   (B) taking
(C) taken   (D) took

Answer: **B、D、A**

❶ 句子意思是「在舉行遊行的前一天夜裡，那兩個騙子讓燈整夜亮著。」have sth. V-ing 這個句型結構表示「使某人／物一直處於某種狀態」，後面常接一段時間。本題句子講述的是過去的事。根據 all night long 可以判斷這裡是要說明燈是整夜都亮著的，表達「使……一直處於某種狀態」，要用 have sth. V-ing，所以答案選 (B)。

❷ 句子意思是「今天早上，我割傷我的手指了。」have sth. V-ed 表示「遭遇或受到某種不幸或意外事故」，但並不著重說明「是什麼使其遭遇這種意外或不幸」。cut 的過去分詞還是 cut，所以應該選 (D)。

❸ 句子的意思是：「我要我弟幫我把垃圾拿出去丟。」此處使用了 have sb. + 原 V 的句型，只有 (A) 為正確答案。

It is/has been + ... + since...

我們常說的「自從你離開家已經三年了。」或「從我開始做這行，已經十年了。」這些句子中都含有「迄今為止一共有多久時間」的意思，所以可以用這個句型來表達。

 關鍵句型 **點**

❶ 這個句型強調的時間段是從過去到現在。主句通常用一般現在式或現在完成式，即「It is/has been＋時間段」，since引導的子句通常用一般過去式。但如果主句強調某動作或狀態是從過去一直持續到現在，那麼since引導的子句則要用現在完成式。

❷ 如果子句中做動詞是延續性動詞，則子句表示「從這個動作或狀態的結束時算起」，所以要翻譯成否定意思，即「有多長時間沒有……了」。

例 How long **has it been since** you were in Beijing?

→你離開北京多久了？

❸ 如果子句中的動詞是瞬間性動詞，則子句表示「從該動作開始的那刻起」，意思順著翻譯即可。

例 **It has been** just a week **since** I arrived here.

→我到這裡剛好有一星期了。

❹ 這個句型可延伸為：「It was＋時間段＋since...」。此時since引導的子句用過去完成式。

會話演練 線

A **It has been** just a week **since** I arrived here.

A: 我到這裡剛好有一星期了。

B You should get on well with your new classmates.

B: 你應該好好地和你的新同學相處。

A How long **has it been** **since** you were in Beijing?

A: 你離開北京多久了？

B Three years.

B: 三年了。

A You look fine today.

A: 你今天看起來氣色很好。

B **It has been** two days **since** I was ill.

B: 我已康復兩天了。

A **It has been** so many years **since** I last met John.

A: 我上次見到約翰已經好多年前了。

B Yeah. He lives so far away.

B: 對啊，他住好遠。

A **It has been** two hours **since** the movie started.

A: 電影已經開始兩小時了。

B If it doesn't end soon I'll have to go to the restroom.

B: 再不趕快結束，我就要去上廁所了。

Level

5

It is/has been ＋ ... ＋ since...

例句 **一連發**

❶ It has been seven years **since** I began to work as a doctor.
自從我當醫生以來已經七年了。

❷ It is/has been six years **since** he came to this school to teach English.
他來這所學校教英文已經六年了。

❸ It was three months **since** she had **begun** to take swimming lessons.
她學了三個月的游泳了。

❹ It has been a long time **since** we met you last time.
從上次之後，我們已經好久沒見面了。

❺ How long **has it been since** you had a rise in salary?
自從你上次調薪已經多久了？

❻ It is/has been two years **since** we began to use this machine.
我們使用這台機器已有二年了。

❼ It has been four years **since** he graduated from college.
他大學畢業到現在已經四年了。

( ) ❶ How long is it _____ you last smoked?
    (A) that   (B) since
    (C) after   (D) when

( ) ❷ How time flies! _____ has been three years _____Ann left her motherland.
    (A) It / since   (B) That / that
    (C) It / before   (D) It / when

( ) ❸ It has been _____ since the man last took a shower.
    (A) a few days   (B) yesterday
    (C) three a.m.   (D) early

Level

5

It is/has been ＋ ... ＋ since...

Answer: **B、A、A**

❶ 句子的意思是「你戒煙多久了？」「It is ＋時間段＋ since ＋ 子句」句型中，子句中的動詞 smoke 是延續性動詞，所以子句 表示「從這個動作或狀態的結束時算起」，要翻譯成否定意思。 另外，其他幾個連接詞 that, after, when 放在句中，意思都不對， 所以正確答案是 (B)。

❷ 句子的意思是「時光飛逝！安離開故鄉已經三年了。」句型「It is/has been ＋一段時間＋ since...」，表示「自從……開始到 現在已有多久了」，所以正確答案是 (A)。

❸ 句子的意思是：「自從這個男人上次淋浴，已經過了幾天了。」 It has been... since... 句型需搭配「時間長度」使用，而非「時 間點」，因此代表「時間點」的 (B)、(C) 都可不考慮；而 (D) 也並非一個時間長度，只有 (A) 為正確答案。

❶ You _____ better _____ soon.
(A) had / to leave
(B) would / to leave
(C) have / leave
(D) had / leave

❷ –_____ are you getting on _____?
–Quite well. Thank you.
(A) How / with
(B) How / X
(C) What / with
(D) What / X

❸ _____ I can understand your idea, but _____ I don't like what you did.
(A) On one hand / on other hand
(B) One hand / other hand
(C) On the one hand / on the other hand
(D) One the one hand / X

❹ _____ I should fail again, I won't give up.
(A) Whether
(B) As if
(C) Even if
(D) Until

❺ The poor man_____.
(A) had his face burn
(B) had his face burning
(C) had his face burned
(D) had burning his face

❻ Don't have her _____ in the rain.
(A) /
(B) wait
(C) waiting
(D) waited

❼ Both she and I _____ interested in rock music.
(A) are
(B) am
(C) is
(D) X

8 Either she or I _____ going to attend the meeting.

(A) are
(B) am
(C) is
(D) be

9 The reason why I was late was _____ my car was broken down on the way.

(A) /
(B) that
(C) because
(D) when

10 It _____ that the painter used his wife as the model in that painting.

(A) says
(B) said
(C) is saying
(D) is said

11 The woman was _____ annoying _____ nobody wanted to be with her.

(A) such / that
(B) so / that
(C) such / for
(D) so / for

12 Carrie is _____ that the men all admire her.

(A) so charming woman
(B) such charming
(C) so charming a woman
(D) such charming a woman

13 I hit him hard, _____ he fell to the ground.

(A) so that
(B) such that
(C) but
(D) in order that

14 They _____ camp in the tent rather than _____ in the dirty inn.

(A) preferred to / they stay
(B) preferred to / staying
(C) preferred to / they won't stay
(D) preferred to / stay

超詳細解析

1 這裡用的是句型You'd better的用法。You'd better 是You had better的縮略形式，其後面要用原形動詞，所以選(D)。

2 首先確認句首疑問詞要用how，而要詢問「某人最近怎麼樣？」直接用「How＋be＋人稱＋getting along/on?」即可，不需要接介系詞with。所以選(B)。

3 這裡用的是句型on (the) one hand,...on the other (hand)。這個句型可以用來引導事情互相矛盾的兩個方面，意思是「一方面……，可是另一方面……」。on the other hand可以單獨使用，但是on (the) one hand不可單獨使用，必須與on the other (hand) 並用。所以選(C)。

4 這裡用的是句型even if...，表達讓步關係。whether是「是否」，as if是「好像」，until是「到……為止」，都不符合句子含義和邏輯關係，只有even if「即使；儘管……」適用，所以選(C)。

5 按正常情理推斷，一個人不可能是自己故意燒傷臉部的，而一定是被什麼燒傷了面部，也就是遭遇了意外事故，句型have sth. V-ed的一個重要用法，就是表示「遭受某種不幸或意外事故」，所以選(C)。

6 句子意思是「不要讓她一直在雨中等待。」句型have sth./sb. V-ing這個句型結構表示「使某人／物一直處於某種狀態。」答案選(C)。

7 both...and...表示「……和……都」。當both...and...連接兩個名詞作主詞時，動詞通常用複數形式。這裡she和I是並列主詞，所以動詞要用複數形式。be interested in的複數形式就是are interested in。答案選(A)。

8 either...or...連接兩個主詞時，動詞在人稱和單複數上必須與它最近的主詞保持一致，也就是「就近原則」。離本題動詞be going to最近的主詞是I，所以它的形式應該與 I 保持一致，即am going to，選(B)。

9 句型The reason why... is that中，關係詞只能用that引導，不能省略，也不能用連接詞because來引導，故正確答案是(B)。

⑩ 句子意思是「據說這個畫家在那幅畫中用他的妻子作為模特兒。」這裡需要用到句型It is/was said＋that子句，意思是「據說……」，表示這個說法的出處來源不清楚或沒必要知道。句首的It在句子中充當形式主詞，動詞要使用被動語態。這裡只有is said 是被動語態，故選(D)。

⑪ 句型so...that和such...that都可以表示「如此……以致」，後面都接that子句。但是不一樣的是：such...that中的such是形容詞，只能修飾名詞；so...that中的so為副詞，可以修飾形容詞或副詞。而本題中annoying就是形容詞，所以正確答案是(B)。

⑫ 這裡要注意的是句型so...that...和such...that...的異同。當that前面是單數可數名詞而且該名詞前面有別的形容詞修飾時，這兩個句型可以互換，即：so＋形容詞＋a/an＋單數可數名詞＋that子句＝such＋a/an＋形容詞＋單數可數名詞＋that子句。根據句型結構可以判斷只有(C)是正確答案。

⑬ so that...可以表示「以便；為了；目的是」。此時，可以與in order that...互換。so that...還可以表示「因此」、「以致」、「結果」。so that引導的子句放在句末時，前面可以用逗號隔開。此時，so that...不能用in order that...代替。而本題的he fell to the ground就是I hit him hard造成的結果，所以答案是(A)。

⑭ 句型prefer to do sth. rather than do sth.用來表示兩者間的選擇，意思是「比較喜歡……，而不喜歡……」；「寧願做……而不願做……」。prefer後面要加to不定詞，而rather than後面則接原形動詞。句子的意思是「他們寧願住帳篷也不願住在那個髒兮兮的旅館。」正確答案是(D)。

Level

5

超詳細解析

過關測驗解答

01~05:(D)(B)(C)(C)(C)　　　　　　　11~14:(B)(C)(A)(D)
06~10:(C)(A)(B)(B)(D)

補充文法面

it 引導的名詞子句，2 類形容詞子句，9 大副詞子句

複合句是相對於簡單句和並列句而言的。當一個句子中的某個成分不是由一個單字或片語充當，而是由一個句子充當時，便構成了主從複合句。所以複合句是由一個主句和一個或一個以上的子句共同構成的句子。主句是整個句子的主體部分，往往可以獨立存在。子句則是整個句子的一個句子成分，不能獨立存在，只能從屬於主句。主句和子句之間通常需要用從屬連接詞、關係代名詞、關係副詞、連接代名詞、連接副詞等來連接。

在句子的幾個成分中，除了述部不可能用子句來充當外，主詞、受詞、補語、關係詞、副詞、同位語等句子成分都可以用子句來充當。依照它們在複合句中的功能，又可以分成名詞子句、形容詞子句和副詞子句。

1 名詞子句

因為主詞、補語、受詞和同位語通常都是由名詞充當，所以主詞子句、補語子句、受詞子句和同位語子句常被統稱為名詞子句。引導名詞子句的包括從屬連接詞（如that, whether, if）、連接代名詞（如who, whom, what, which, whose）、連接副詞（如when, where, why, how）；從屬連接詞只能連接主句和子句，而連接代名詞和連接副詞除了具連接作用外，還可充當子句中的句子成分。

其中需要特別說明的是：主詞子句中出現和使用頻率很高的一種，就是it引導的主詞子句。由於主詞子句位於句首顯得過於頭重腳輕，所以通常用it作虛主詞，而將真正的主詞子句移至句子後面。由it引導的主詞子句常見於以下一些句型中：

★ It is＋動詞過去分詞(said, reported, believed...)＋that子句

例：It is said that there is a fairy in the forest.
　　據説這個森林裡有一個精靈。
　　It's reported that 5 people were killed in the big fire.
　　據報導，這次大火中有五個人喪生。

★ It is＋形容詞(clear, true, necessary, possible...)＋that子句

例：It is clear that your plan is doomed to failure.
　　很明顯地，你的計畫註定要失敗。
　　It is quite necessary that we should learn English and
　　computer skills well.
　　我們應該把英文和電腦技能學好，是相當必要的。

★ It is＋名詞(a pity, a shame, a fact...)＋that子句

例：It is a pity that you missed the movie.
　　你錯過了這場電影真遺憾。

2 形容詞子句

　　用來修飾名詞、代名詞或名詞片語的子句稱為形容詞子句，也就是我們所説的關係子句。被關係子句修飾的詞叫先行詞。關係子句放在先行詞後面，用關係代名詞（如that, who, whom, which, whose）或關係副詞（如when, where, why）來引導。關係代名詞和關係副詞的作用不僅是把主句和子句連接起來，還要在子句中充當一個句子成分。根據關係子句與先行詞的密切程度，關係子句又可以分為限定性關係子句和非限定性關係子句兩種。

　　1.限定性關係子句：

　　限定性關係子句是其所修飾的先行詞不可缺少的關係詞，如果去掉這一子句，先行詞的意義就會不明確，主句的意思也會不完整。主句和子句之間一般不可以用逗號隔開。

例：The man who/that you met just now is my boss.
你剛才碰見的那個人是我的老闆。
That is the reason why she quit the job.
這就是她辭職的原因。

2.非限定性關係子句：

非限定性關係子句與其所修飾的先行詞的關係不密切，只是對先行詞作一種補充說明。如果去掉這一子句，主句的意思仍然清楚而不會受影響。主句和子句之間要用逗號隔開。另外，非限定性關係子句不可由關係代名詞that引導。

例：Nancy has five children, four of whom are boys.
南茜有五個孩子，其中四個都是男孩。
He drank too much, which made his wife angry.
他喝了太多酒，讓他的妻子很生氣。

3 副詞子句

在子句中充當副詞，修飾主句中的述部動詞、形容詞和副詞等，被稱作副詞子句。引導副詞子句的詞多是從屬連接詞。從屬連接詞只能連接主句和子句，不能充當句子的成分。副詞子句如果位於句首，通常用逗號與主句隔開，如果位於句尾，通常可以不用逗號隔開。

根據副詞子句在句子中的作用，又可以分為時間副詞子句、地點副詞子句、原因副詞子句、結果副詞子句、目的副詞子句、方式副詞子句、條件副詞子句、讓步副詞子句、比較副詞子句等九種。

1.時間副詞子句：

引導時間副詞子句的從屬連接詞有when, while, as, before, after, until, till, since, as soon as, whenever等。另外，在時間副詞子句中，通常用現在式代替未來式。

例：He'll go home as soon as the class is over.
　　課程一結束，他就要回家。

2.地點副詞子句：

引導地點副詞子句的從屬連接詞有where,wherever, anywhere 等。

例：Where there is life, there is hope.
　　哪裡有生命，哪裡就有希望。

3.原因副詞子句：

引導原因副詞子句的從屬連接詞有because, as, since, now that, for, considering that, seeing that等。

例：As it is snowing, I dare not drive the car.
　　因為在下雪，所以我不敢開車。

4.結果副詞子句：

引導結果副詞子句的從屬連接詞有so that, such that, so...that, such...that等。其中需要特別注意的是so...that與such...that。句型「so＋形容詞＋a(n)＋可數名詞單數＋that...」與句型「such＋a(n)＋形容詞＋可數名詞單數＋that...」可以相互轉換。但是當such修飾的是可數名詞複數或不可數名詞時，兩個句型就不能互換。

例：It's so cold a day that we don't want to go out.
　　=It's such a cold day that we don't want to go out.
　　今天那麼冷，我們不想出去。
　　They are such cute dogs that I want to take them home.
　　（○）這些小狗這麼可愛，我要把牠們帶回家。
　　≠They are so cute dogs that I want to take them home.
　　（×）

5.目的副詞子句：

引導目的副詞子句的從屬連接詞有so that, in order that, for fear that, lest, in case that等。在目的副詞子句中，述部動詞前通常用情態動詞can, may, could, will, might, would, should, shall等。另外，目的副詞子句多位於主句之後。其中需要特別注意的是：so that既可以引導結果副詞子句，也可以引導目的副詞子句。

例：Mary helped John study English so that he could pass the exam.
瑪莉幫助約翰學習英文，以便讓他能夠通過考試。
I will work hard in order that my family may be happier.
為了讓家人更幸福，我要努力工作。
Please remind me in case I forget.
請提醒我，以免我忘了。

6.方式副詞子句：

引導方式副詞子句的從屬連接詞有as, as if, as though等。

例：Please do the experiments as the teacher told you.
請按照老師告訴你們的方式做實驗。
She behaves as if/as though she were a child.
她的行為舉止就像是一個孩子。

7.條件副詞子句：

引導條件副詞子句的從屬連接詞有if, unless, in case, if only, as long as, so long as, providing that, on condition that等。條件副詞子句還分成真實條件副詞子句（表示符合客觀事實的情況）和非真實條件副詞子句（表示與事實相反或違背說話人意願的假設情況）；前者要用陳述語氣，後者要用虛擬語氣。例如「If only＋條件子句＋主句」的句型，就會分這兩種情況。

例：If you make a promise, you will keep it.
如果你做出了承諾，你就要遵守它。
We are happy as long as you are happy.
只要你快樂，我們就快樂。
Take an umbrella in case it (should) rain.
帶把傘吧！以免下雨。
If only you would work a little harder.
要是你能再努力一點工作就好了！（虛擬語氣）

8.讓步副詞子句：

引導讓步副詞子句的從屬連接詞有though, although, even if, even though, whatever, however, no matter what, no matter how, whether...or等。

例：He looks young though he is sixty.
雖然他六十歲了，但看起來很年輕。
Even if I know the truth, I won't tell her.
就算我知道事情的真相，我也不會告訴她。
However busy my parents are, they will spend some time with me. 不管我父母再怎麼忙，他們也會抽空陪我。

9.比較副詞子句：

引導比較副詞子句的從屬連接詞有as, as...as, than, not as/so...as等。還有一種口語中比較常見的句型是「The＋比較級，the＋比較級 」，「表示 越……越……」。

例：He is a little fatter than before. 他比以前胖了一點。
The new theater is two times as large as the old one.
這個新劇場是舊劇場的兩倍大。
The older the man, the more experienced he will be.
人越老，經驗就越豐富。

Level 6

我們常說「你應該在中午前交出報告。」或「我應該為這件事情負責。」這些句子中都指出了「應該……」，所以可以用這個句型來表達。

關鍵句型 **點**

❶ 這是一個被動語態句型，可以用來表示勸告、建議、義務、責任等。主詞通常是人，有時也可以是物。suppose要以被動形式出現，後面接不定詞。這個句型的常見時態有現在式、過去式、現在進行式、過去進行式幾種。

❷ 最常見的是be supposed to do sth.意為「應該做某事」，表示主詞被期望或被要求做某事。相當於should do sth.。

 You **are supposed to** sign the official papers in ink.
→你應該用鋼筆簽署這些正式文件。

❸ 其否定形式be not supposed to do sth. 則可以表達一種建議或勸告，更常用來表示主詞不被允許或禁止做某事，是一種委婉的禁止，意為「不應該做某事」。

 You **are not supposed to** set up campfires and pick flowers here. →你們不應該在這裡生營火和摘花。

❹ 另一個用被動語態形式表示「禁止」、「不許」的句型是：be not allowed ...和be forbidden...。這個句型的主詞如果是人，allowed和forbidden後面通常接不定詞to do sth.，即：sb. be not allowed/forbidden to do sth.；主詞如果是事情，allowed後面可以不接其他語詞，因為sth. be not allowed/forbidden本身就是完整的句子結構了。

會話演練 線

會話翻譯

A You **are supposed** to sign the official papers in ink.

B Sorry, I forgot.

A: 你應該用鋼筆簽署這些正式文件。

B: 對不起，我忘了。

A What **are** you **supposed to** do now?

B I am **supposed to** copy the material for you.

A: 你現在應該做什麼？

B: 我現在應該影印這份資料給你。

A You **are not supposed to** set up campfires and pick flowers here.

B Thank you for your reminding.

A: 你們不應該在這裡生營火和摘花。

B: 謝謝你的提醒。

A Is it all right to smoke here?

B No, smoking **is forbidden/ is not allowed** here.

A: 可以在這裡抽煙嗎？

B: 不行，這裡禁止抽煙。

be (not) supposed to...

265

例句 **一連發**

❶ You **are supposed to** support your parents.
你應該資助你的父母。

❷ She **is supposed to** arrive at school at eight o'clock.
她應該在八點鐘到學校。

❸ You**'re supposed to** ask the teacher if you want to enter the lab.
如果你想進實驗室，應該先問問老師。

❹ We **are not supposed to** talk about others' private affairs.
我們不應該談論別人的隱私。

❺ We **are supposed** to help each other.
我們理應互相幫助。

❻ He **was supposed to** get here at nine.
他本應該九點鐘到這裡。

❼ You **were supposed to** be working at that time.
那個時候，你應該是在工作。

❽ I **am allowed to** watch TV for an hour every day.
我被允許每天看一個小時的電視。

❾ Mixed race marriages **were forbidden** by law.
以前法律禁止異族通婚。

小小試身手

( ) ❶ We _____ supposed to _____ at six. But we are late.
(A) are / arrive
(B) are / be arriving
(C) will be / be arriving
(D) were / arrive

( ) ❷ You _____ at home every day.
(A) are not supposed to stay
(B) were not supposed to stay
(C) are not supposed staying
(D) were not supposed staying

Answer: **D、A**

❶ 句子的意思是「我們本應該六點鐘就到達的。但是我們遲到了。」be supposed to do sth. 表示「應該做某事」。這個句型的過去式 was/were supposed to do sth. 常常用來將過去本應該做或發生的事與實際發生的事情進行對照，可譯為「本應該」。根據題目的最後一句 But we are late. 可以判斷「我們六點鐘到達」是過去應該做的事，所以要用 were supposed，答案選 (D)。

❷ 句子的意思是「你不應該天天待在家裡。」這裡用的是句型 be not supposed to do sth.，意為「不應該做某事」。在這裡表達的是一種建議或勸告。根據 every day 可以判斷這裡要用 be not supposed 的現在簡單式，所以答案是 (A)。

It seems/seemed that/as if...

「這看起來似乎事有蹊蹺。」或「這似乎太離奇了。」，這些句子中都含有揣測的意思，表示「表面上看起來好像……」這時就可以使用這個句型。

 關鍵句型 **點**

❶ 在「It seems/seemed＋that子句」這個句型中，seem表示「看起來」，後面接的是that引導的子句。這是一個表示猜測或判斷的句型，意思是「看來……；似乎是……；好像……」。

例 **It seemed that** he was a bit angry.
→看起來他好像有點生氣了。

❷ 如果要表示「在某人看來，似乎是……」，則要在seem後加上 to sb.，即：It seems/seemed to sb. that...。

例 **It seems to me that** you are always lying.
→在我看來，你一直在撒謊。

❸ 另外，再告訴大家一個非常相似的句型：It appears/appeared (to sb.) that子句。這個句型也表示「在（某人）看來，好像……」的意思。

例 **It appears that** she likes sweet food very much.
→看來她好像很喜歡吃甜食。

❹ 在「It seems/seemed as if子句」這個句型中，seem後面接as if引導的子句，當表示真實情況時，用陳述語氣；否則就用虛擬語氣。

例 **It seemed as if** I couldn't think of a word to say.
→當時，我似乎想不出一個恰當的字眼來。

會話翻譯

A He went out without saying a word.

B It **seemed that** he was a bit angry.

A: 他沒有說一句話就出去了。

B: 看起來他好像有點生氣了。

A **It seems to me that** you are always lying.

B Oh, no. I think you misunderstand me.

A: 在我看來，你一直在撒謊。

B: 哦！不。我想你誤會我了。

A You should have scolded him.

B At that time, **it seemed as if** I couldn't think of a word to say.

A: 你當時應該責備他。

B: 當時，我似乎想不出一個恰當的字眼來。

A **It appears that** she likes sweet food very much.

B So she has many decayed teeth.

A: 看來她好像很喜歡吃甜食。

B: 所以她有很多蛀牙。

Level

6

It seems/seemed that/as if...

269

例句 **一連發**

❶ **It seems (that)** he was late for the train.
看來他沒搭上火車。

❷ **It seems that** American fast food is the most popular in the world.
看來美國的速食是世界上最受歡迎的。

❸ **It seems to me that** they should answer for this.
在我看來，他們似乎應該為此事負責。

❹ **It seemed that** no one knew what happened.
看來沒有人知道發生了什麼事。

❺ **It appears that** you were wrong.
看來你好像錯了。

❻ **It appears to me that** he wants to teach us all he has.
在我看來，他似乎要把他所會的都教給我們。

❼ **It seems as if** he were in a dream.
看來他像是在做夢。

❽ **It seems as if** she knew this man.
看來她好像認識這個人。

❾ **It seems as if** our team is going to win.
看來我們隊伍要獲勝了。

❿ **It looks as if** it is going to rain.
看起來好像要下雨了。

( ) **❶** ____ to me that you object to my suggestion.
(A) It is seems (B) It is seemed
(C) You seems (D) It seems

( ) **❷** It seems ____ she were ten years younger.
(A) to (B) that
(C) as if (D) X

( ) **❸** It _____ that more than one of these people are lying.
(A) seems to (B) seems to me
(C) appears to (D) appears as

Level

6

Answer: D、C、B

❶ 句子的意思是「在我看來，你反對我的提議。」「It seems to sb. that...」句型中，引導詞要用 it，所以答案選 (D)。

❷ 句子的意思是「看起來她好像年輕了十歲。」「It seems as if...」句型中，seem 後面可以接 that 引導的子句，也可以接 as if 引導的子句。但是 It seems as if... 句型常可以用來表示不可能實現的非真實情況，此時要用虛擬語氣。根據句意和子句中的 were 可以判斷這句是虛擬語氣，所以要用 as if，答案選 (C)。

❸ 句子的意思是：「看來這些人不只一個在說謊。」seems to、appears to 後面都必須加上名詞，因此只有 (B) 為正確答案。

It seems/seemed that/as if...

Unit 03 It's (high/about) time that...

我們常說的「你該去寫作業了」或「我該去買雙新鞋了」，這些句子中都表示「做某事的時機到了」，這時就可以使用這個句型來表達。

 關鍵句型 **點**

❶ 句型「It is (about/high) time＋that...」是個常用句型，that引導的是子句，表示「該做⋯⋯的時候了」，而實際上是意味著「早該做某事而沒有做」，所以子句需用虛擬語氣來傳達一種遺憾、急迫、批評、抱怨等情緒，多是在催促某人儘快做某事。子句的動詞形式要用過去簡單式。有時，about和high可以省略。

例 **It's about time** you bought a new car.
→你該買輛新車了。

It's high time you made up your mind.
→你該做決定了。

It's time we ordered dinner.
→我們該點晚餐了。

會話翻譯

A Wait a minute. Why I couldn't start my engine?

B **It's about time** you bought a new car.

A: 稍等一下。為什麼我發動不了引擎？

B: 你該買輛新車了。

A **It's time** we ordered dinner.

B Let's wait for Tom a little longer.

A: 我們該點菜了。

B: 讓我們再多等湯姆一下子吧。

Level

6

A **It's high time** you made up your mind.

B But I want to think all the choices over.

A: 你該做決定了。

B: 但是我想再把所有的方案好好考慮一下。

A Don't you think **it's high time** we head home?

B Just give me another three minutes.

A: 你不覺得我們差不多是時候該回家了嗎？

B: 再給我三分鐘。

It's (high/about) time that...

例句 一連發

❶ It is time (that) we had classes.
我們該上課了。

❷ It is high time (that) the weather improved.
天氣真該好起來了。

❸ Don't you think **it's about time** we went home?
你不認為我們應該回家了嗎？

❹ It's time that we took action and did our bit for the AIDS patients.
我們該採取行動為愛滋病人盡一份心力了。

❺ It's high time that we did something to improve our environment.
我們該為環保做些事情了。

❻ It's about time I had my hair cut.
我該剪頭髮了。

❼ It's high time that he was taught a lesson.
現在該是他學到教訓的時候了。

( ) ❶ You are very selfish. It's high time you ＿＿＿ that you are not the most important person in the world.
(A) realized (B) realize
(C) have realized (D) will realize

( ) ❷ It is about time that you ＿＿＿ down to business.
(A) must get (B) got
(C) getting (D) will get

( ) ❸ It's about time that you ＿＿＿ ready for the interview.
(A) getting (B) gotten
(C) got (D) to get

Answer: **A、B、C**

❶ 句子的意思是「你太自私了。你該瞭解到你並不是世界上最了不起的人物。」句型「It is (high/about) time (that)...」意為「該是……的時候了」。這個子句需要用虛擬語氣，動詞用過去式 realized，所以答案選 (A)。

❷ 句子的意思是「該是靜下心來處理事務的時候了。」這個句型的子句需要用虛擬語氣，動詞用過去式 got，所以答案是 (B)。

❸ 句子的意思是：「是時候你該為面試做好準備了。」此處使用的是 be about time that sb. + 過去式的句型，必須選擇唯一的原形動詞 (C) 為正確答案。

do nothing but do...

我們常說的「我們除了空等，什麼事也不能做」
或「他只是出一張嘴，什麼事也沒做」，這些句子
中都強調「只有……，其他一概沒有」，所以可以
用這個句型來表達。

關鍵句型 **點**

❶ 在do nothing but do sth.句型中，but後面要接原形動詞。意思為
「除了做……外，什麼也不做」或「別無選擇，只能……」。

例 I could **do nothing but sit** here.
→我只能坐在這裡等了。

例 She **does nothing but complain** about her fate.
→她只是抱怨自己的命不好，什麼事也沒做。

❷ 另外，還有一個類似的句型：have nothing to do but do sth.「除
了做……之外，無事可做」；have no choice but to do sth.「除
了做……外別無選擇」。

例 I **have no choice but to do** so.
→除此之外，我別無選擇。

會話演練 **線**

會話翻譯

A Linda always misses good opportunities.

B She **does nothing but complain** about her fate.

A: 琳達總是錯過好機會。

B: 她只是抱怨自己命不好，什麼事也沒做。

A I could **do nothing but sit** here.

B Sorry. Please wait for me a little longer.

A: 我只能坐在這裡了。

B: 對不起，請再多等我一下子。

A Why are you doing that?

B I **have no choice but to do so**.

A: 你為什麼要做這樣的事呢？

B: 除此之外，我別無選擇。

A The cat **does nothing but** sleep.

B That's why I love her so much.

A: 這貓除了睡覺以外什麼也不做。

B: 所以我才愛牠啊。

Level

6

do nothing but do...

例句 **一連發**

❶ I can **do nothing but let** him know.
我能做的只有告知他。

❷ I **have nothing to do but sit** down and read the newspaper.
我除了坐下來看報紙之外，無事可做。

❸ I **did nothing but write** letters all day.
我一整天除了寫信什麼事也沒做。

❹ He could **do nothing but wait** with patience.
他除了耐心等待，什麼事也不能做。

❺ I **had no choice but to call** in the police.
我別無選擇，只能請警察來。

❻ I **had no choice but to wait** for help.
我別無選擇，只能等待救援。

❼ We **have no choice but to believe** you.
除了相信你，我們別無選擇。

❽ You **have no choice but to follow** me.
你除了跟著我別無選擇。

小小試身手

( ) **❶** Lots of empty bottles were found under the old man's bed. He must have done nothing but _____.
(A) drink
(B) to drink
(C) drinking
(D) drunk

( ) **❷** The man did nothing but _____ back what he had said.
(A) taken
(B) took
(C) toking
(D) take

( ) **❸** I could do nothing but _____ as the tornado came closer.
(A) watch
(B) watched
(C) saw
(D) seeing

Answer: **A、D、A**

❶ 句子的意思是「在那位老人的床下發現了許多空瓶，他一定除了喝酒外什麼事也沒有做。」句型 do nothing but do sth. 表示「除了做……外，什麼事也不做」。nothing but 後面要接原形動詞，所以答案選 (A)。

❷ 句子的意思是「除了收回他所說的話，那個男人什麼也沒做。」句型 do nothing but do sth. 中的 nothing but 後面要接原形動詞，所以答案選 (D)。

❸ 句子的意思是：「我什麼也做不了，只能眼睜睜看著龍捲風越來越近。」此處使用的是 can do nothing but + 原 V 的句型，只有 (A) 為正確答案。

Unit 05 no matter ＋疑問詞…

　　我們常說的「不管發生什麼事，我都會陪在你身邊。」或「無論你說什麼，我都不相信。」，中文裡的「不管……」、「不論……」、「無論……」等，都可以用這個句型來表達。

關鍵句型 點

❶「no matter＋疑問詞」意思是「無論……」、「不論……」，可以用來引導讓步子句。其中的疑問詞可以是疑問代名詞也可以是疑問副詞。根據疑問詞的不同，又可分為以下幾個句型：

　・no matter who/whom...... 表示「無論誰……」。
　・no matter what .... 表示「無論什麼……」。
　・no matter which.............. 表示「無論哪一個……」。
　・no matter how .... 表示「無論怎樣……」。

 Try to take it easy, **no matter what** happens.
　　→無論發生什麼，都要試著放鬆。

❷ 另外，「疑問詞＋ -ever」相當於「no matter＋疑問詞」，ever本是一個加強語氣的字，加在疑問詞後面，不僅使疑問詞的語氣加強，而且變成具有讓步意義的一個複合詞，所以由「疑問詞＋-ever」構成的句型「疑問詞＋-ever＋…」也表示「不管……都……」，可以與句型「no matter＋疑問詞＋…」互換。即：

　・no matter what ＝ whatever　　・no matter who ＝ whoever
　・no matter when ＝ whenever　　・no matter where ＝ wherever
　・no matter which ＝ whichever　　・no matter how ＝ however

 The singer is always popular **wherever** she goes.
　　→這個歌手不管到哪裡，總是受到歡迎。

會話翻譯

A I'm too nervous to think.

B Try to take it easy, **no matter what** happens.

A: 我太緊張了，無法思考。

B: 無論發生什麼事，都要試著放鬆。

A The singer is always popular **no matter where** she goes.

B But I have never heard of her. Why?

A: 這個歌手不管到哪裡，總是受到歡迎。

B: 但是我沒聽説過她。為什麼？

Level

6

no matter ＋ 疑問詞…

A All my CDs are here. You may borrow **whichever** you like.

B It's very kind of you.

A: 我所有的 CD 都在這裡。你想借哪張就借哪張。

B: 你人真是太好了。

A We must finish the job, **no matter what**.

B Yeah, the fate of the world lies in our hands now.

A: 無論如何，我們都要完成這個任務。

B: 沒錯，世界的命運就掌握在我們手上了。

❶ **No matter which** you may choose, you'll be pleased.
=**Whichever** you may choose, you'll be pleased.
無論你選哪一個，你都會滿意的。

❷ **No matter what** happened, we would support you.
=**Whatever** happened, we would support you.
無論發生了什麼事，我們都會支持你的。

❸ **No matter who** you are, you must obey the law.
=**Whoever** you are, you must obey the law.
不管你是誰，你都要守法。

❹ I will miss you **no matter where** I am.
=I will miss you **wherever** I am.
不管我在哪裡，我都會想念你。

❺ I'll help you **no matter when** you get into trouble.
=I'll help you **whenever** you get into trouble.
無論什麼時候你碰到麻煩，我都會幫你。

❻ **No matter who** you may be, you have no right to do such a thing.
不論你是誰，你都無權做這樣的事。

❼ **No matter how** hard the job may be, I will finish it.
無論這個工作有多難，我都會完成它。

❽ She is willing to help you **however** busy she is.
無論多忙，她都願意幫助你。

( )❶ _____ much advice I gave him, he did exactly what he wanted to do.
(A) How   (B) Whatever
(C) However   (D) No matter

( )❷ I've got three copies of this book. I'll give one to _____ asks for it.
(A) anyone   (B) whomever
(C) whoever   (D) no matter who

( )❸ No matter _____ knocks on the door, do not open it unless you're sure it's me.
(A) how   (B) who
(C) whom   (D) where

Level

6

no matter ＋疑問詞…

Answer: **C、C、B**

❶ 句子的意思是「無論我給他多少勸告，他卻完全按照他所想的去做。」這裡用的是句型「no matter ＋疑問詞＋……」以及「疑問詞＋ -ever ＋……」的用法。根據句子的意思和邏輯關係，知道第一句是個讓步子句。而 how 只能引導名詞子句，不能引導讓步子句。however 相當於 no matter how 引導讓步子句，意思是「無論怎樣」，符合題意，所以答案選 (C)。

❷ 句子的意思是「這本書我有三本。我會給任何需要它的人一本。」anyone 不能引導句子，而 no matter who 只能引導讓步子句，不能引導受詞子句。空格中要填的應該是後面子句的主詞，而 whomever 是受詞，不是主詞。所以答案應該選 (C)。

❸ 句子的意思是：「無論是誰敲門，只要不是我，就不要開門。」能夠做出敲門動作的只有「人」（也許機器也可能敲門，但選項中沒有出現 what），且因為是做出敲門動作，而非被敲，因此也不能使用受詞 whom，這裡只有 (B) 為正確答案。

283

Unit 06

Not until...

我們常說的「不到緊要關頭，絕不放棄。」或「直到父親去世，他才了解父親對他的愛。」這些句子中都強調「到某個時間點才做某事」，所以可以用這個句型來表達。

 關鍵句型 **點**

❶ 這個句型相當於...not...until...，表達的意思是「直至某時才做某事」。這個句型中，until和not連在一起，放在句首。此時，主句必須部分倒裝，即動詞放在主詞的前面。但是切記子句並不需要變動，不必倒裝。其具體結構為：「Not until＋子句＋助動詞＋主句主詞＋...」。

例 **Not until** she took off her sunglasses **did I** realize she was a film star.

→直到她摘下墨鏡我才意識到她是個電影明星。

❷ 同時需要記憶的是句型Not until...的強調句型是：「It is/was not until＋子句＋that＋... 」。這時就不能使用倒裝句型了。

例 **It is not until** one is ill **that** he realizes the value of health.

→直到生病時，一個人才瞭解到健康的價值。

會話翻譯

A Did you know the woman you met was a film star?

B **Not until** she took off her sunglasses **did I** realize she was a film star.

A: 你知道你碰見的那個女人是個電影明星嗎？

B: 直到她摘下墨鏡我才意識到她是個電影明星。

A Are you feeling better?

B Yes. Thank you. **It is not until** one is ill **that** he realizes the value of health.

A: 你感覺好點了嗎？

B: 是的，謝謝。直到生病時，一個人才瞭解到健康的價值。

A **Not until** well into the night **did** he come back.

B He should have a good rest today.

A: 他直到深夜才回來。

B: 他今天應該好好休息一下。

A How did you figure out your boyfriend was cheating on you?

B **Not until** I saw him kissing a boy **did** I realize I wasn't his only one.

A: 你怎麼發現你男友劈腿的？

B: 直到我看到他在親一個男生，才發現原來我不是他的唯一。

例句一連發

❶ Not until the early years of the 19th century **did men** know what heat is.
直到 19 世紀初，人類才知道熱能是什麼。

❷ Not until he informed me of this **did I** know it.
直到他把這件事告訴我，我才知道。

❸ Not until the teacher came in **did we** stop talking.
直到老師進來我們才停止講話。

❹ It was not until then **that** she told me the truth.
直到那時，她才告訴我事情的真相。

❺ Not until I entered the meeting room **did I** realize that I had left the papers at home.
直到進了會議室我才意識到我把文件放在家裡了。

❻ It was not until bedtime **that** he remembered to take the medicine.
直到睡覺時他才想起要吃藥。

❼ It is not until you promise to help her **that** she will go away.
一直要等到你答應幫她，她才肯離開。

小小試身手

( )❶ It was _____ yesterday _____ I was wrong.
    (A) until / did I realize
    (B) not until / did I realize
    (C) until / that I realized
    (D) not until / that I realized

( )❷ Not until _____ work _____ how much time she had wasted.
    (A) she began to / she realized
    (B) did she begin to / did she realize
    (C) did she begin to / she realized
    (D) she began to / did she realize

Answer: **D、D**

❶ 句子的意思是「直到昨天我才意識到我錯了。」這是 not until 的強調句型，連接詞要用 that。此時，句子不需要倒裝，所以答案選 (D)。

❷ 句子的意思是「直到開始工作她才意識到她浪費了多少時間」。「Not until ＋子句＋助動詞＋主句主詞＋ ...」這個句型的意思是「直至某時才做某事」。此時，主句必須部分倒裝。因為這個句子是過去時態，所以倒裝時要在主句主詞的前面加上助動詞 did，後面再接原形動詞，但是子句並不需要倒裝。答案選 (D)。

What if...?

我們所說的「要是沒有你，我們該怎麼辦？」
或「如果我們拿不到那筆錢呢？」或「萬一這個世
界上只剩下你一個人，你怎麼辦呢？」，這些句子
都隱含了「設想未知情況」的意思，可以用這個句
型來表達。

 關鍵句型 **點**

❶ What if ...?是個省略用法的句型，意思是「如果……將會怎麼
樣？」「要是……的話，怎麼辦？」這個句型的完整結構應該
是：What are you going to do if...? 或What will/would happen
if...?。省略形式的句型What if...?在口語中十分常見。

例 **What if** the weather there turns out cold?
→如果那邊天氣變冷了怎麼辦？

❷ What if ...?句型還可以引出一個建議、邀請或要求。If子句多用
現在簡單式，但有時為了使建議、邀請或要求婉轉一些，也會
用過去式。

會話演練

會話翻譯

A Don't put too many clothes in my suitcase.

A: 不要在我的行李箱裡放那麼多衣服。

B **What if** the weather there turns out cold?

B: 如果那邊天氣變冷了怎麼辦?

A **What if** I don't buy the camera for you?

A: 如果我不買這台相機給你,你怎麼辦?

B I will save money to buy it myself.

B: 我會自己存錢買下它。

A We should wait for him a little longer.

A: 我們應該多等他一下下。

B **What if** he doesn't come?

B: 如果他不來的話怎麼辦?

A There's no need to bring an umbrella.

A: 不需要帶傘。

B But **what if** it rains?

B: 可是如果下雨怎麼辦?

A **What if** the dog is pregnant?

A: 如果那隻狗懷孕了怎麼辦?

B Then we'll ask if our friends want puppies.

B: 那我們就問朋友們要不要小狗。

例句 **一連發**

❶ What if he gets home before us and can't get in?
要是他在我們之前趕到家而又進不去呢？

❷ What if you were to run out of money? What would you do?
要是你把錢花光了呢？你要怎麼辦？

❸ What if your parents don't agree?
如果你的父母不同意呢？

❹ What if you should fall sick?
要是你生病了怎麼辦？

❺ What if World War III should happen?
要是發生第三次世界大戰怎麼辦？

❻ What if you join us for lunch?
跟我們一起吃午餐怎麼樣？

❼ What if we move your bookshelf to that room?
我們把你的書架搬到那個房間怎麼樣？

小小試身手

( )❶ ____ if aliens ____ the earth?
(A) How / invade
(B) What / will invade
(C) How / don't invade
(D) What / should invade

( )❷ –I decide to go boating by myself.
–_____ a storm comes up?
(A) Why
(B) What will happen if
(C) What are you going to do if
(D) What happens when

Answer: **D**、**C**

❶ 句子的意思是「如果外星人侵入地球怎麼辦？」What if ...? 是個省略用法的句型，意思是「如果……將會怎麼樣？」「要是……怎麼辦？」If引導的子句內容實際上是不太可能發生的，所以要用虛擬語氣，動詞用 should invade，答案選 (D)。

❷ 句子的意思是「我決定一個人去划船。」「要是發生暴風雨怎麼辦？」what if 是個省略結構，它相當於 What are you going to do if...? 或 What will/would happen if...? 而根據題目中第一個人所說的話，我們可以知道這裡的 what if 想表達的完整意思應該是 What are you going to do if a storm comes up?，所以答案選 (C)。

If only...

我們常說的「我要是能住在別墅裡該有多好啊！」或「如果可以再見到他就好了」或「要是時光能倒流就好了」，這些句子都說明了一種「美好的假設情況」，所以可以用這個句型來表達。

關鍵句型 點

❶ 句型「If only＋條件子句(＋主句)」是if only引導的一個既有子句又有主句的完整結構，常可以譯為「只要……就……」。其中的if是連接詞，only是用來強調語氣的。這個句型主要用在虛擬語氣中，用以表達強烈的願望或非真實條件。

例 If only she could have lived a little longer.
　→要是她能活得再長一些，那該多好啊！

❷ If only...引導的條件子句用於虛擬語氣時，有時態的變化：
　·當表示與現在事實相反的願望時，動詞用：were/過去式動詞。

例 If only I were as clever as you!
　→要是我像你一樣聰明該多好啊！
　·當表示與過去事實相反的願望時，動詞用：had＋過去分詞。

例 If only the ambulance **had arrived** in time.
　→要是救護車及時趕到就好了。
　·當表示與現在或未來事實相反的願望時，動詞用：would/could＋原形動詞。

例 If only she **would marry** me! →她要是能嫁給我該有多好！

A What a big fine house it is!

B **If only** this was my own house.

A: 多麼漂亮的大房子啊！

B: 要是這是我自己的房子該有多好！

A I have solved all the riddles.

B **If only** I were as clever as you!

A: 我已經解開了所有的謎語。

B: 要是我像你一樣聰明該多好啊！

A **If only** the ambulance had arrived in time.

B It's too late now.

A: 如果要是救護車及時趕到就好了。

B: 現在已經太遲了。

A I was pretty much broke earlier this year.

B **If only** you'd let me know earlier, I would have helped.

A: 我今年初幾乎破產了。

B: 如果你早點告訴我，我就會幫你了。

A **If only** I could be rich without working!

B Life doesn't work that way.

A: 如果我可以不用工作就有錢，那有多好啊！

B: 人生不是這樣子的。

Level

6

If only...

293

例句**一連發**

❶ If only we were well-prepared, we would have climbed up to the mountain peak.
要是我們有做好準備，我們就可以爬到山頂的。

❷ If only you had told me that, I wouldn't have done it.
要是你早點告訴我，我就不這麼做了。

❸ If only she had another chance, she would do better.
要是她再有一次機會，她就會做得更好。

❹ We could surely have overcome these difficulties **if only** we were closely united.
要是我們有緊密地團結一致，本來能克服這些困難的。

❺ If only I had had more money, I would have bought more books.
要是那時我有更多的錢，我就會多買幾本書了。

❻ If only they were still alive!
他們要是還活著多好啊！

❼ If only I didn't have to work for a living.
要是不必為謀生而工作就好了。

❽ If only you would listen to reason.
要是你能聽得進道理就好了。

❾ If only we didn't have so much homework!
我們要是沒有那麼多作業該多好啊！

小小試身手

( ) ❶ ＿＿＿ you do your best, you ＿＿＿.
    (A) If only / will succeed
    (B) If only / succeed
    (C) Only if / will succeed
    (D) Only if / succeed

( ) ❷ –Did you see Beckham just now?
    –Oh, no. If only I ＿＿＿ here earlier!
    (A) came   (B) would come
    (C) am coming   (D) had come

Answer: **A、D**

❶ 句子的意思是「要是你竭盡全力，你就會成功。」句型「If only ＋條件子句＋主句」，意思是「只要……」、「只要……就……」。only if 也可以引導條件子句，意思是「除非……才……」、「必須有……（條件），才能……」only if 強調的是條件，且置於句首時，後接的子句要倒裝，而 you do your best 並沒有倒裝，所以排除 (C)、(D)。「If only ＋條件子句＋主句」常用來表達願望或非真實條件，子句動詞既可以用陳述語氣，也可以用虛擬語氣。我們根據題目句子的意思可以判斷，透過努力取得成功並不是無法實現、遙不可及的願望。所以答案選 (A)。

❷ 句子的意思是「你剛才見到貝克漢了嗎？」「噢！沒有。如果我早點到這裡就好了。」If only 引導一個條件子句單獨出現時，常用於感嘆或直接表達惋惜、願望等，可以譯為「要是……該多好」、「真希望……」、「但願……」。根據對話內容可知，回答者沒有看到貝克漢，正因為如此，他才會說「如果我早點到這裡就好了」。也就是說他認為如果我早點到就可能看到這個國際巨星了。所以 if only 後面的子句要用虛擬語氣，而且要用過去式的虛擬語氣，此時，動詞要用「had ＋過去分詞」。所以答案是 (D)。

1 I will be waiting for you here _____ you come.

(A) no matter when   (B) no matter whenever

(C) no matter who   (D) no matter

2 It _____ their decision _____ changed by what had happened.

(A) seemed as if / would never be

(B) seemed as if / would never have been

(C) is seemed / would never be

(D) is seemed as if / would never have been

3 He _____ supposed to come to attend the meeting. What's happened?

(A) X   (B) is

(C) was   (D) had

4 If only I _____ my car.

(A) lost   (B) didn't lose

(C) had lost   (D) hadn't lost

5 I'm afraid I have to go now. It's time I _____ and _____ my little daughter.

(A) go / pick up   (B) must go / pick up

(C) went / picked up   (D) will go / pick up

6 I can do nothing but _____ you well.
- (A) wish
- (B) to wish
- (C) wishing
- (D) I wish

7 What if _____ a dinosaur?
- (A) you meet
- (B) you should meet
- (C) your meeting
- (D) you will meet

8 Hardly had the singer finished her performance _____ the audience gave her a huge applause.
- (A) and
- (B) when
- (C) than
- (D) as soon as

9 Scarcely _____ in the city when _____ .
- (A) they settled down, the hurricane came
- (B) they settled down / the hurricane would come
- (C) had they settled down / the hurricane came
- (D) had they settled down / came the hurricane

10 Not until the early years of the 17th century _____ the existence of the Far East.
- (A) Europeans did know
- (B) Europeans knew
- (C) didn't Europeans know
- (D) did Europeans know

11 _____ a robber _____ your house, what would you do?
- (A) Supposed, to break into
- (B) Supposed / will break into
- (C) Suppose / breaking into
- (D) Supposing / should break into

❶ 這裡要注意的是句型「no matter＋疑問詞＋……」以及「疑問詞＋-ever ＋……」的用法。兩個句型都表示「不管……都……」，所以可以互換。句子的意思是「無論你什麼時候來，我都在這裡等你。」no matter who是「無論是誰」，不符合題意，所以選(A)。

❷ 句子意思是「他們的決定似乎不會因為發生的事而改變。」句型「It seemed as if＋子句」中的seem後面接as if引導的子句。根據by what had happened判斷，seem後面接的as if子句用了虛擬語氣表示對過去既成事實的假設，所以as if子句的動詞形式應該用would never have been來對應。答案為(B)。

❸ 句型be supposed to do sth. 表示「應該做某事」。根據題目最後一句What's happened?可判斷這裡講述的是過去的事，所以應該用was/were supposed to do sth.，可譯為「本應該」。答案選(C)。

❹ If only引導一個條件子句單獨出現時，常用於感嘆或直接表達惋惜、願望等感情色彩時，可以譯為「要是……該多好」、「真希望……」、「但願……」。因為丟車是已經發生的事，所以if only後面的子句要用虛擬語氣，而且要用過去式的虛擬語氣。此時，動詞要用「had＋過去分詞」形式。而且說話人當然不可能希望丟了車，所以had lost是不合理的，要用否定形式hadn't lost，答案選(D)。

❺ 句型「It is time (that)...」的意思是「該是……的時候了」。這個句型的動詞通常用過去式，這並不是表示事情發生在過去，反而表示現在或未來的概念。這其實是虛擬語氣的用法，即用來表示說話人的想法、意願和情緒，說明說話人希望儘快發生或早該發生。正確答案選(C)。

❻ 這裡用的句型do nothing but do sth.，意思是「除了做……外什麼也不做」。but後面要用原形動詞，即wish。整句話的意思是「我除了祝福你，什麼也做不了。」正確答案是(A)。

❼ What if ...?是個省略用法的句型，意思是「如果……將會怎麼樣？」「要是……怎麼辦？」。本題意思是「如果你碰見一隻恐龍怎麼辦？」顯然這實際上是不太可能發生的，因為恐龍已經滅絕了。所以if子句要用虛擬語氣，動詞用should meet，答案選(B)。

8 句型「Hardly/Scarcely＋had＋主詞＋過去分詞＋（子句）＋when/before＋過去式動詞」中,子句的引導詞要用when或before,所以選(B)。

9 這裡用的是「Scarcely＋had＋主詞＋過去分詞＋（子句）＋when/before＋過去式動詞」句型,scarcely表示「幾乎不」,具有否定含義。hardly或scarcely置於句首時,主句要用倒裝結構,即動詞要提前;而子句不需要倒裝。答案是(C)。

10 句子的意思是「直到17世紀初,歐洲人才知道遠東的存在」。句型「Not until＋時間＋助動詞＋主句主詞＋……」的意思是「直至某時才做某事」。主句的主詞和述部必須部分倒裝。本題要借助表示過去時態的助動詞did,再接原形動詞know,所以選(D)。

11 句型Suppose/Supposing (that)...。可以表示非真實條件,用虛擬語式表示對現在或將來的假設。本題是在假設和虛擬一個情景:「如果強盜闖入你的家裡,你會怎麼辦?」這是個對將來可能發生事情的假設,所以動詞用虛擬形式should break into,正確答案選(D)。

Level

6

超詳細解析

過關測驗解答

01~06: (A)(B)(C)(D)(C)(A)　　　　　07~11: (B)(B)(C)(D)(D)

Level 6
補充文法面

倒裝句

是一種語法手段，或由於句子結構的要求或由於強調某一句子的需要。根據述部放在主詞前面的情況，倒裝又分為完全倒裝和部分倒裝。

1 完全倒裝

將整個述部放在主詞之前的倒裝叫做完全倒裝。

例：How goes the time? 幾點鐘了？
　　Here comes the bus. 公車來了。

2 部分倒裝

將述部中的一部分（如助動詞、情態動詞或連綴動詞等）放在主詞之前的倒裝叫做部分倒裝。

例：Never have I been the city before.
　　我以前從沒有來過這座城市。

3 句子結構的倒裝

常見的句子結構倒裝有以下幾種情況：

1.用於各種形式的疑問句中。

例：Are you from America?（你是美國人嗎？）；
　　Who is that girl?（那個女孩是誰？）；
　　Has he set off already?（他已經出發了嗎？）

2.用於here, there, away, up, down, out, in, now, then等開頭的句中。此時的述部動詞通常是go, come, be, follow...等。這種倒裝常常用於更生動地描寫一個情景。

例：There goes the bell. 鈴響了。
　　Away went the old woman. 那個老婦人離開了。
　　Up went the arrow into the air. 箭朝上射進了天空。

3.用於there/here be句型中。

例：There are many pigeons on the square.
　　廣場上有許多鴿子。
　　There lived an pretty girl in the village.
　　那個村子裡住著一位美麗的女孩。
　　Here are some apples.
　　這裡有一些蘋果。

4.用於祝福語中。

例：May you succeed! 祝你成功！
　　May you be happy! 祝你幸福！

5.用於as等引導的讓步副詞子句中。

例：Child as he is, he knows a lot.
　　儘管他還是個孩子，但是他懂得很多。
　　Cold as the weather was, it couldn't cool our enthusiam for work.
　　儘管天氣很冷，但卻不能澆息我們的工作熱情。

6. 用於某些省略了if的虛擬條件句中（通常是以had, were, should等開頭）。

例：Were I you, I would accept his invitation.
    如果我是你，我就會接受他的邀請。
    Had I had time, I would go.
    如果我有時間，我就會去。
    Should anyone call, tell him to come to my office.
    萬一有人來找我，請他到我的辦公室來。

7. 當so, neither, nor等副詞放在句首時，全句需要倒裝，由此，構成兩個對話中常見的句型：「so＋連綴動詞/助動詞/情態動詞＋主詞」和「neither/nor＋連綴動詞/助動詞/情態動詞＋主詞」。

例：If you can finish the job, so can I.
    如果你能完成這項工作，我也可以。
    I didn't go to the party last night, nor did Alice.
    我昨晚沒有去參加派對，艾莉絲也沒有去。

8. 當never, seldom, nor, hardly, little, not sooner...等表示否定的副詞或連接詞放在句首時，全句需要倒裝。

例：Seldom did my mother argue with others.
    我的母親很少和別人爭論。
    Hardly did I think it possible.
    我幾乎認為這是不可能的。

▷4 強調需要的倒裝

強調句子中的某個成分時，就會將其移至主詞之前，構成倒裝。

1.強調述部

例：No longer is he working in that company.
　　他已經不在那間公司上班了。（強調No longer）
　　Return I dare not!
　　我不敢回去呀！（強調Return）

2.強調補語

例：Child as she is, she knows a lot.
　　儘管她還是個孩子，但她懂得很多。（強調Child）
　　Moving is the story!
　　這個故事真感人！（強調Moving）

　　Right in the first page is the article of mine.
　　第一頁就是我的文章。（強調Right in the first page）

3.強調受詞

例："What's your name?" asked my teacher.
　　「你叫什麼名字？」我的老師問。
　　（強調 "What's your name?"）
　　"Wait for me here please," said Tom.
　　「請在這裡等我。」湯姆說。
　　（強調 "Wait for me here please."）
　　All this we must take into account.
　　這一切我們都必須再次考慮。（強調All this）

5▷ 強調副詞

例：Just then along came the policemen.
　　就在那時，警察趕到了。（強調Just then）

原來如此 系列 E239

英文句型完全搞定：初學者也能馬上學會的點線面致勝法

用點線面致勝法，從掌握基礎國高中英文句型開始！

作　　　者	曾韋婕◎著
顧　　　問	曾文旭
社　　　長	王毓芳
編輯統籌	耿文國
主　　　編	吳靜宜
執行編輯	吳佳芬、廖婉婷、黃韻璇
美術編輯	王桂芳
法律顧問	北辰著作權事務所　蕭雄淋律師、幸秋妙律師

初　　　版	2020年12月
出　　　版	捷徑文化出版事業有限公司
電　　　話	（02）2752-5618
傳　　　真	（02）2752-5619

定　　　價	新台幣340元／港幣113元
產品內容	1書

總 經 銷	采舍國際有限公司
地　　　址	235新北市中和區中山路二段366巷10號3樓
電　　　話	（02）8245-8786
傳　　　真	（02）8245-8718

港澳地區經銷商	和平圖書有限公司
地　　　址	香港柴灣嘉業街12號百樂門大廈17樓
電　　　話	（852）2804-6687
傳　　　真	（852）2804-6409

▶本書部分圖片由 Shutterstock、freepik 圖庫提供。

捷徑 Book站

現在就上臉書（FACEBOOK）「捷徑BOOK站」並按讚加入粉絲團，
就可享每月不定期新書資訊和粉絲專享小禮物喔！

http://www.facebook.com/royalroadbooks
讀者來函：royalroadbooks@gmail.com

國家圖書館出版品預行編目資料

英文句型完全搞定：初學者也能馬上學會的點線
面致勝法 / 曾韋婕著. -- 初版. -- 臺北市：捷徑文
化, 2020.12
　　面；　公分（原來如此：E239）
ISBN 978-986-5507-49-7(平裝)

1. 英語　2. 句法

805.169　　　　　　　　　　　　　　109017875